ULTIMATE SUBMISSION

A collection of twenty erotic stories

Edited by Miranda Forbes

Published by Accent Press Ltd – 2007
ISBN 1905170963 / 9781905170968

Copyright © Accent Press Ltd 2007

All rights reserved. No part of this book may be reproduced, stored in a retrieval system, or transmitted in any form or by any means, electronic, electrostatic, magnetic tape, mechanical, photocopying, recording or otherwise, without the written permission of the publishers: Accent Press Ltd, PO Box 26,
Treharris, CF46 9AG

Printed and bound in the UK by
Creative Print and Design, Wales

Cover Design by
Red Dot Design

Also available from Xcite Books:

Sex & Seduction	1905170785	price £7.99
Sex & Satisfaction	1905170777	price £7.99
Sex & Submission	1905170793	price £7.99
5 Minute Fantasies 1	1905170610	price £7.99
5 Minute Fantasies 2	190517070X	price £7.99
5 Minute Fantasies 3	1905170718	price £7.99
Whip Me	1905170920	price £7.99
Spank Me	1905170939	price £7.99
Tie Me Up	1905170947	price £7.99
Ultimate Sins	1905170599	price £7.99
Ultimate Sex	1905170955	price £7.99
Ultimate Submission	1905170963	price £7.99

www.xcitebooks.com

Contents

Reunion	Beverly Langland	1
Web Of Desire	Emily Dubberley	15
The Silken Web	Virginia Beech	27
Lot Twenty-One	Andrea Carver	39
Public Exposure	Cathryn Cooper	46
Personal Shopper	Izzy French	54
Waiting For A Spanking	Shanna Germain	62
Sparring Partners	Everica May	69
Possession	Penelope Friday	76
The Gift	Dolores Day	86
The Gatecrasher	Stephen Albrow	96
All Right On The Night	Jo Nation	106
Fairground Attraction	Mimi Elise	117
Rodeo Girl	Matt Pascoe	124
The Boss	DMW Carol	131
Man-Stalker	Landon Dixon	138
His Lordship's New Mistress	Virginia Beech	148
Company Policy	Emily Dubberley	164
The Hole In The Oak-Panelled Wall	Roger Frank Selby	169
The Collaring of Camilia	Alexia Falkendown	180

Reunion
by Beverly Langland

It was a reunion of sorts, although Sarah didn't recognise any of her classmates. Paula, her ex schoolmistress was nowhere to be found. It seemed that she too had moved on. With the absence of a familiar face, Sarah felt estranged and out of place, even after the effort she had made. Even so, she still hoped to recapture the excitement she once felt. Maybe she nurtured unrealistic expectations. Perhaps too much water had passed under the bridge after all. She scanned the room once again. The eyes held the same need but the faces had aged or been replaced by younger, fresher ones. Still, the old school gymnasium hadn't changed much, even after all this time. The lingering smell brought back happy memories, evoked the sense of belonging that so eluded her.

Not that Sarah had the right to complain. She had made her choices, and in the main was happy. She had married since her last attendance, was now the mother of two lovely young girls, had even managed a successful career despite of that. Outwardly, Sarah had fulfilled every goal. Perhaps too quickly, too easily. Now she lacked ambition, had lost her zest for life. When the emptiness grew too great she had to remind herself that she lived a comfortable, contented lifestyle – had the love of her family. Yet, it was the feeling of contentment that so scared her. She was still young after all. She should be travelling the world, living life to the full.

Of course, other things had changed. She had put on more than a few pounds for one, carried with her heavier emotional baggage, felt shackled by the same success she once craved. After the demands of career and family she had little energy for herself. In short, Sarah felt tied and tired. So it came that Sarah decided to take a short but deserved break. Each year she received an invitation to the *School Reunion*. Each year she threw the envelope into the refuse unopened. This year she accepted. Sarah realised going back was a risk, knew she had a propensity to filter bad experiences, to remember only the good. She felt the risk worth taking. So she slipped on her school uniform, determined to recapture the past. Though her resolve was fading fast. It had been so long ago – a different time, a different world to the ordered existence she now lived. She mingled in the crowd, uncomfortable and alone, the waistband of her short pleated skirt strangling her determination. Although it wasn't the biting pain she found most discomforting. It was something less tangible – the burden of guilt she carried. She had deceived her husband, had told him she was on a business trip when in fact she was in search of… Sarah shook her head – she didn't know what exactly.

Sarah felt guilty also for her need to attend, for donning clothes more suited to her elder daughter. A thirty-year old woman dressed in school uniform may be interpreted many ways, none of them flattering Sarah decided. She knew dressing like a young girl was provocative, overtly sexual – especially here. Part of her needed to recapture her youth, to feel sexual once more. The ruse worked. She could feel eyes staring – ogling – men, women, boys, girls, pupils, teachers. Some of the older schoolmasters even paused, blatantly sizing her up before spotting her pink form badge and moving on, disappointment written on their faces.

Although Sarah enjoyed the attention she recognised the real thrill was her feeling of renewed freedom – of not being mother, wife, boss, chief-cook and bottle-wash. For one night at least she could put aside family and friends – responsibility of any kind. She needed to lose herself in the past. She had even tied her fine blonde hair into bunches, donned a brand new pair of white panties, changed expensive tights for socks – had figuratively wiped the slate clean, become a virgin once more. Dressing this way had been a cathartic experience. Yet, the need to do so frightened her. For a long time afterwards she dare not leave her hotel room, and when at last she gained courage enough, only under cover of a raincoat.

In the school gymnasium she felt less exposed. Eyes were less condemning here, faces less judgemental. She was approached many times, talked to people of all persuasions keen to get to know her. At first Sarah felt flattered, then, as her popularity became evident her former confidence returned. She had almost forgotten how wonderful it felt to be wanted. For now at least, it didn't matter by whom. The desire of some was obvious. A twinkle in the eye, a bulge in a trouser leg, a whisper in her ear. Sarah politely declined all offers, not wishing to offend, but once she had reaffirmed her desirability she felt no need – was uncertain at least – whether to take matters further.

Spotting Jadine made up her mind. Sarah felt her arousal grow the instant she saw the schoolmistress approach. Something in her stride, in her confident manner told her *she* was the one. Her clothes – the tight pencil skirt, the button-down jacket – were as clichéd as her own. The simplicity of the contrast appealed to Sarah. There was no doubt they were meant for each other, were of the same mind. Just watching Jadine move made Sarah tremble, her whole demeanour reeked of authority. Her dark hair was tied back in a tight bun making her face appear a little harsh, yet there was kindness in her eyes. Sarah initially thought – hoped perhaps – that the woman was older, but it became obvious as she drew near that Jadine was close to her own age. It also became obvious that she was in no mood for frivolity. "Name?"

"Sarah, miss."

"Such a pretty girl. Why haven't I seen you here before?"

Sarah hesitated. "I've been away miss."

Jadine gave Sarah a quick appraisal, spotted her wedding ring, smiled knowingly. Foolishly, when Sarah changed she couldn't bear to remove it. The sentiment was misguided, for now Jadine already knew too much about her. "I see you're married."

"Yes miss."

"Children?"

Sarah felt the blood drain from her face. Her children belonged to another world – one in which she didn't lie, didn't deceive, didn't crave the company of strangers. She didn't want to be reminded of her betrayal. The woman shouldn't of asked, had no right to ask. Jadine caught Sarah's hesitation. "Never mind! How old are you?"

"Fifteen miss." At such times Sarah was always fifteen.

Jadine raised an eyebrow. "Fifteen? Was that a good age for you Sarah? Perhaps you had a *special* friend?"

"Yes miss."

"You may dispense with the formality."

"Yes miss."

Jadine smiled, perhaps sensing that Sarah needed to play the anxious teenager. She looked Sarah over a second time, lingering this time, reappraising. Sarah hoped appreciating. "Your husband doesn't suspect?"

"Oh no miss."

"Isn't that deceitful? Why don't you engage him?"

"I couldn't! He wouldn't understand and besides I'm..."

"...in Form B." Jadine fingered Sarah's badge.

Sarah did her best to look Jadine in the eye. "Yes miss."

"My, what a dilemma. How on Earth do you cope?"

Sarah blushed, the blood rushing back to her cheeks as quickly as it had drained earlier. Masturbation is always a poor substitute but in times of need it was the only recourse she had. Jadine must have spotted the sadness reflected in Sarah's eyes for her manner changed. She stroked Sarah's cheek. "Has it been so very long?" Tears welled to Sarah's eyes. She felt suddenly ashamed of her weakness, of her deceit, of the denial of her own needs. Jadine took her hand, patted it affectionately. "Well, we shall have to set you straight." She removed a card from her jacket pocket.

"Can't we do it now?"

Jadine froze in surprise and Sarah felt her cheeks burning in shame. Her sudden outburst sounded much too needy. Yet, she only had one night of freedom. "Now?" The dark-haired woman looked puzzled.

"Please miss. I have a room."

"Is that wise? You know nothing about me, nor I you."

Of course Jadine was right. It was a mark of Sarah's desperation that she even considered placing her trust in this stranger. Yet, she needed her – so badly that any sense of reason, any sense of right or wrong had left her completely. "I'll pay," she added hurriedly.

Jadine's eyes turned suddenly dark and Sarah saw then the danger, the violence that set the two of them apart, that made them a perfect match. "I'm not a prostitute and I resent the implication," Jadine spat. For a moment her eyes locked on Sarah's, their lingering menace making Sarah tremble. If anything, the air of danger stoked Sarah's arousal, made her want Jadine more. She bowed her head, set her mouth in a little girl pout, seducing Jadine the best she knew how. "Sorry miss. It's just that I can't go back without... without..."

Jadine took her in her arms. "Oh, you pathetic child."

Her face smothered against Jadine's bust, Sarah smiled to herself. It seemed that Jadine wasn't immune to her schoolgirl charm. She looked up, her eyes pale and watery. "Please miss, I'll be a good girl."

"It seems that *I* now have a dilemma Sarah. I know I shouldn't agree but I'm concerned you'll do something stupid if I don't."

"Then you'll come to my room?"

"Yes, I'll go with you, but I shall make you pay for the inconvenience."

"Oh thank you miss, thank you!"

The short drive to the hotel was fraught with tension. Both women chose to remain silent, Sarah growing ever more apprehensive. Once her initial euphoria had passed she was beset with worry. Had she made too hasty a decision? She glanced often at Jadine when she thought the woman wasn't paying attention. Was she truly taking Jadine back to her hotel room? There was a time when she would not have been concerned. But now…

She was still questioning her sanity when they entered the hotel room. Sarah's mobile phone beeped in the darkness. She refused to acknowledge it's warning, hastily turned it off, placed it in a bedside drawer. She deliberately hadn't phoned home and her husband would be concerned, or hopelessly out of his depth with the girls. Though she conceded that the message could be from any number of people. Someone, somewhere was always calling out to her. Sarah couldn't think of that now. Not now! She didn't have the strength, the energy – the will.

She turned, stood facing Jadine while the dark-haired woman removed her jacket. Jadine took her time, folded it neatly, precisely. Sarah made good use of the opportunity to appraise. Her eyes were drawn to Jadine's large breasts.

Free of the confines of her tight jacket they seemed to have grown. And now she had time to look, Jadine's bottom appeared more rounded. To Sarah's mind Jadine's figure gave her the perfect matronly appearance. She had to resist the urge to rush to the safety of Jadine's arms, to tear open the woman's blouse, to curl up and suckle while Jadine held her close. Sarah knew Jadine would offer her that and more, but before comfort came chastisement. It was the currency of their world. Jadine looked up, noted Sarah watching. She pointed to the corner of the room. "Hands on heads!"

Sarah did as instructed without question, without wondering about the absurdity of her response. She stood in the corner facing the wall, placed her hands on her head. Jadine stepped up behind, so close Sarah could feel the heat of her body. "I see you *have* played this game before." She tapped Sarah's legs further apart with the side of her foot. It was only a small adjustment but it served its purpose – let Sarah know who was in charge. "Before we proceed Sarah, I will explain my rules." She ran a trail down Sarah's arm with her fingernail, unaware of the Goosebumps rising on Sarah's skin. "Firstly, I shall punish you for your deceit, for your insolence in bringing me here. I do not like infidelity in my girls. Therefore your punishment will be harsh. It may have been some time for you Sarah, so I make no bones that it will hurt." She paused, touched Sarah's bottom. "You understand this?"

"Yes miss."

"The truth is I shall enjoy hurting you." Sarah shifted uncomfortably. "You seem anxious. Don't you want me to hurt you?"

"No miss."

"Good. I wouldn't want to encourage you to deceive again. After your punishment you will thank me with your tongue." Jadine leaned in close to Sarah's ear. "I want to feel your pretty mouth on my cunt. If you work diligently I may allow you to pleasure yourself, although that is by no means certain."

Sarah held her breath as she listened to Jadine's calculated description of events to follow, made all the more menacing for the measured softness of her voice. She dare not breathe for fear of fainting, was already feeling dizzy. Was this what she was searching for? Would Jadine's abuse, her humiliation in the woman's hands fill the void? "Now's the time to speak up if you have doubts."

Sarah remained silent while Jadine moved away, sat on the edge of the bed. "Come here." Sarah approached with trepidation, stood trembling by Jadine's side.

"Are you wearing panties?"

"Yes miss."

"Are they wet?"

"Soaking miss."

"Well, young lady remove them. Isn't it time you showed me your pussy?"

Sarah discreetly removed her panties. Then spotting Jadine's look of disapproval, she raised the front of her skirt, took perverse pleasure from the humiliation of exposing herself inches from this stranger's face. "Such a pretty little thing." Eyes fixed on Sarah's, Jadine ran a finger deftly between Sarah's bloated labia, raised the coated fingertip to her mouth and licked it clean. She smiled, patted Sarah's thigh. "Oh well, down to business. Lie across my lap Sarah. Let me see what all the fuss is about."

Sarah offered no resistance. She lay across Jadine's lap obediently, head down to one side, her thighs straight out behind – then waited. Jadine shifted her weight, leaned forward. Sarah could feel the warmth of the woman's heavy breasts pressing against her. Jadine ran her hands over the silky cheeks of Sarah's rear. As she stroked, Sarah felt her excitement grow in line with her anticipation.

She was taken aback by the force, the ferocity of the first blow. She cried out in shock. Pain flared across her buttocks, warm and wonderful. She had expected more foreplay, but Jadine seemed intent on getting on with the job at hand. Sarah squirmed in Jadine's lap, a vain attempt to avoid the heavy blows which followed in quick succession. Jadine pinned her tight, held her arms in a lock so she couldn't fight. Jadine had warned her that she would not hold back and the woman kept true to her word. Pain seared across Sarah's backside, her skin burning as the fierce heat failed to dissipate. Tears welled to her eyes and before long she sobbed openly.

If Jadine noticed Sarah's misery she paid no heed. If anything, she continued the spanking with increased gusto. There was little respite – a short pause, a change of focus. After a short while Sarah's beating became a ritual dance as Jadine smacked first one bottom cheek and then the other. Despite the pain, thrilling, masochistic tremors surged through Sarah. Her chastisement was harsh – harsher than any punishment she had hitherto received – yet she was determined to endure. This was the penance she had come in search of. Her atonement for years of denial.

Jadine seemed equally determined to break her. She slapped hard and regularly, and as she did Sarah slipped into an adoring state of worship for her. It was always thus for Sarah. A love of persecution transformed into love for her persecutor. Pain transformed into pleasure. While her bottom burned her pussy grew bloated and wet. It was not unknown for her to climax in the hands of an experienced mistress. This time tough, she fought to hold back, seeking the clarity of pain, raising her bottom in anticipation of the next strike.

Jadine, spotted the signs – stopped – depriving Sarah of any sense of control. She parted Sarah's legs, kneaded her sore and burning flesh until Sarah's pussy was ablaze with desire. Jadine's fingers slipped inside easily, made Sarah jerk and moan. Then they were gone and Jadine continued the spanking at her pace, her fingers occasionally skirting the wetness of Sarah's sex, reminding her of her prize. Soon the poor girl was kicking her legs as Jadine found the limit of Sarah's endurance, momentarily crossed it. Sarah became a burning mass of crimson flesh, her buttocks hot and pain-filled, her pussy a steaming swamp.

For a long while Sarah lay still in Jadine's lap. Both women breathing hard from the exertion of their struggle. Then Jadine's hands were back on Sarah's bottom. She applied lotion to the scorched skin, rubbing the cool liquid into the soft flesh. Occasionally she added Sarah's own wetness by delving a slender digit between the crevice of Sarah's distended pussy lips. Sarah whimpered, focused on the soothing massage, content now to let Jadine bring her to orgasm. Though it did not come quickly. Jadine surprised her, landed another blow to her buttocks. More gentle this time – teasing even. This was a new torture for Sarah. Drawn out pleasure with a sudden injection of pain, the timing of Jadine's spasmodic spanking masterful. Each time Jadine caught Sarah unawares, successive blows taking Sarah closer to the release her body craved. Yet, the timing was Jadine's alone. Sarah became Jadine's plaything, dancing to the beat she dictated.

And Jadine seemed in no hurry to free her captive, intent perhaps on prolonging Sarah's torment. Sarah lost all sense of how long she lay there. It didn't matter. She felt warm and safe draped across Jadine's knees, even as Jadine beat her. All the pressures of her hectic life were forgotten. She wanted nothing more than to wrap herself into the heavy bosom of this matronly woman. Sarah closed her eyes, pleased – content even – that Jadine derived pleasure from her discomfort. She parted her legs, pressed her sex into Jadine's lap, offered herself, waiting for the next hit. When it came, it was low, a little harder, the tips of Jadine's fingers catching Sarah's pussy squarely. A shockwave shot through her, sent alarm signals to her throbbing clitoris. She couldn't take much more of this bittersweet torture, she needed release, needed Jadine to fuck her, hurt her, it didn't matter which. They both led to the same thing in the end. The next blow was equally low, elicited the same response. Sarah spread her legs wider, inviting Jadine to strike again. She got her wish. Jadine caught her fully along the length of her pussy. All at once the intensity became too great, Sarah's orgasm – building for so long – ripped through her body. She convulsed uncontrollably, only vaguely aware of Jadine calling out that she was a *bad girl* as she rained blows upon Sarah's jerking backside. Sarah was lost in her own perverse world – a world where pain and pleasure went hand in hand.

By the time Sarah's orgasm subsided, she lay spent and exhausted across Jadine's lap, her backside searing with pain. She winced as a blob of cooling lotion landed on her bottom, sucked heat from her raw flesh. Tears welled to her eyes as the harshness of her punishment gradually filtered through. The pain rapidly replacing the pleasure she had experienced only moments before. "Please, no more…"

"No more," Jadine agreed, though she continued to rub lotion onto Sarah's bottom. It was only after some time that Sarah realized Jadine seemed to pay particular attention to her anus. Jadine ran her fingertip around the puckered rim, sending tingles up Sarah's spine. Without warning Jadine inserted the tip of her finger, the lubrication allowing it to slip in easily. Sarah was about to protest when the fingertip was withdrawn as quickly as it entered. She had never allowed anyone to venture there, not even her husband, yet it was not unpleasant, especially in the afterglow of her orgasm.

Time and again Jadine penetrated Sarah's virgin hole.

Each time her finger ventured further, sometimes lingering to wriggle and explore. Sarah had never thought of her back passage as sexual, but she started to enjoy Jadine's constant probing. Probing which got deeper with each visit. After a while Sarah surprised herself by pressing her bottom rearwards each time Jadine's finger approached, encouraging Jadine to explore deeper. The invasion into her anus was alien – exciting. She wanted more! Even when Sarah felt the full length of Jadine's finger buried inside her, it wasn't enough. She wriggled and clenched her buttocks, an attempt to keep the finger inside longer. Then, to Sarah's delight, Jadine did not withdraw her finger completely. Instead, she slowly started to frig...

Sarah was just becoming accustomed to this new degrading form of pleasure when she felt her blouse torn open, felt fingers reaching for her breasts, felt tugging on her neglected nipples. The force of Jadine's play a little harsh but in perfect timing with the rhythm of her finger as it worked its way into Sarah's tight hole. In the space of a few minutes, Sarah's excitement had once again reached boiling point and her clitoris screamed out in jealous neglect. She reached for her throbbing button only to have Jadine slap her hand away. The nipple tugging stopped long enough for Sarah to realise just how savagely they had been attacked. Suddenly, Jadine turned Sarah's face towards her and Sarah was met with the sight of Jadine's large breasts. Sarah took a nipple into her mouth without being asked and sucked on it eagerly, rolling her tongue around its considerable length.

Sarah sucked more of Jadine's breast into her mouth, tentatively reached under her skirt and pressed a hand into her crotch. It was a bold move on Sarah's part for she had not been given permission. As soon as Sarah's fingers touched her clitoris she started to spasm. Jadine responded, pumped Sarah's arse with a ferocity to match the tremors rampaging through her body, making Sarah's breasts swung to and fro as she bucked in response to the increased tempo of Jadine's finger-fucking. Her sudden ardour sent Sarah over the edge, her cries filling the room.

It took Sarah some time to recover, after which Jadine removed the offending finger, gingerly rolled Sarah onto the bed. Sarah lay as if in a dream, her body battered and abused, her mind floating around the room in search of its owner. Suddenly, Jadine had Sarah by the hair, was pulling her up the bed, guiding her between her spread thighs. She was naked now, her own excitement obvious. "My turn," she said huskily. Sarah's only thought was to thank her mistress, yet she barely had time to utter *Yes miss* before she was engulfed in the darkness of Jadine's sex.

Sarah awoke late morning, a little disorientated in the unfamiliar room, the space beside her vacant. Jadine had risen early, leaving behind crumpled sheets and the aftertaste of her sex in Sarah's mouth. Sarah felt thankful Jadine had not stayed. It avoided the awkwardness that was sure to exist. She looked at her watch, panicked. If she was quick she just had time to make the office before driving Amy to her swimming class. She bounded out of bed, wincing at the pain in her lower body. She could see in the mirror that she was heavily bruised, would have difficulty concealing them. It was the price she had to pay for her duplicity. She had been unfaithful to her husband and it was difficult to reconcile her actions. She felt exhilarated and wretched at the same time. Yet, the oppressive weight that hung over her had lifted, and by the time she had showered and dressed Sarah had organised her day, planned the evening meal, had even written a shopping list.

She packed her clothes, was tempted to throw the school uniform into the waste basket – stopped herself. It was not so easy to discard. She held up the skirt. Maybe she could let the waist out? Or better yet, loose a few inches. Yes, she would exercise more, lose weight. Sarah grew excited by the challenge, mentally setting herself goals. She would start a new regime.

It was only after she had finished packing that she spotted Jadine's card. Sarah picked it up, considered it – threw it in the waste basket – retrieved it. Why not? Most of her friends spent time at a health spa. A little therapy now and again would do her good. After all, it was no more than her family deserved.

Web Of Desire
by Emily Dubberley

I felt her before I saw her. You know that sensation that you're being looked at? The prickle at the back of your neck that makes you feel uncomfortable for a reason you can't quite place, until you make eye contact and see it wasn't your imagination.

When I realised what was happening, I smiled at her in a 'Do I know you?' way. I didn't recognise her – she was tall, slim and dressed in a slinky, black frock that emphasised her hourglass figure. I was certain I'd have remembered her. I felt a rush of blood to my cock as she shifted her weight from one stiletto-clad foot to the other and I noticed her dress was slashed to the thigh on both sides, revealing a hint of stocking. She didn't smile back, making me worry that she hadn't been looking at me at all, and it was my own lust leading my imagination.

She strode towards me, a glint in her eyes, and I was half-expecting a slap for my errant erection. Her first words did nothing to reassure me.

"You're scared of me."

There is no right answer to an opening line like that. If I disagreed, I'd be suggesting that she was wrong – never a good introduction to a stranger. If I said yes, I'd sound like a wimp. I settled on taking a nonchalant drag of my cigarette and giving her a slightly dorkish smile.

"A lot of people are," she continued. "So, what are you doing here?"

This was more familiar and comfortable ground. Traditional small-talk. Being a regular at media parties, I considered it one of my specialities.

"I'm a friend of Tom's – he lived next door to me when we were kids. You?"

"I hate all this media shit. I just come here to keep my wanker radar updated. I like to keep up to date with what's being talked about at all the fashionable parties to make sure I never accidentally find myself talking about something 'zeitgeisty'"

I smiled again, unsure of what to say, but still aroused to my surprise. She was clearly a woman who knew her own mind – not my usual type at all. As a film producer, I'm used to wannabe actresses trying to get into my pants in the hope it will get them a part. I don't encourage it but, as Tom says, "It's a perk of the job. Take it where you can get it, mate." As such, my usual companions are in their early twenties, with pert breasts and adoring gazes. Some of them are quite bright too, but I'd be lying if I said it was their intelligence that attracts me.

The stranger looked me up and down before meeting my eyes directly, her green eyes glinting in the dim and smoky room.

"I'm leaving. You coming?"

"Err, why?" The question was out of my lips before I engaged my brain.

"You were standing on your own. You didn't mention work in your opening line. That makes you more interesting than anyone else here. And…" she glanced down at my crotch "you seem pleased to see me."

Without waiting for my answer, she turned on her heel and headed to the cloakroom.

I stood there for a few seconds, trying to register what

had just happened. As my brain whirred, I noticed a curvy young thing I vaguely recognised – Linzi, Tammi...something cute and with an 'i' on the end of it – heading towards me. I knew it'd be the same old same old – giggling, hair flicking and 'I love your work', culminating in a lacklustre casual sex session that left me wondering why the morning after, and screening my calls for a week. The mystery woman had intrigued me. I turned my back on – that was it, Sammi – stubbed my cigarette and squeezed through the crowd to catch her at the door.

"You're an astute man," she commented, as I joined her. Oh, for the security of a cigarette to hide behind. I had to answer.

"You seem more interesting than that crowd," I said.

"I didn't mean for leaving them," she said. "I meant for being scared of me."

I was tempted to head back into the familiar throng for a non-threatening night of drink and flirtation, but my cock led me through the door, onto the strangely calm city street.

Outside the party, she was friendlier, with a dark sense of humour that had me laughing despite feeling disconcerted. We walked, talked, and rejected all the bars we passed as unsuitable – or rather, she did. When we got to a quiet street, she said: "This is me. Coming in?"

"Do you usually invite strange men into your house?"

"Only ones who are high profile enough that I could make a fortune by selling my story to the papers if they give me any grief."

Again, the spikiness – but I was getting used to it by now.

"Consider me warned," I laughed, as she unlocked the door.

I wasn't sure what to expect of her flat but the cosy

bookshelf-lined room I was presented with wouldn't have been my first assumption.

"Drink?" she asked, getting two tumblers out and filling them with ice before I could answer.

"I'll have what you're having."
"And I thought you knew your own mind," she said, pouring a hefty measure of Jack Daniels into both our glasses. She bent over and slipped off her heels, giving me a tantalising glimpse of her tight, round arse before she stood up and walked over to me with the drinks.

"Well, sit down then. I won't bite."

I bit back the obvious response. Something told me I'd need to work a bit harder with her.

"So, tell me about you – and skip the media bullshit," she said, curling up in a large and battered leather sofa, and patting the cushion next to her. On her own turf and without the heels, she seemed less threatening, but I still didn't feel comfortable enough to remove my own shoes, and sat upright next to her, as I began to do as she'd asked.

Four hours later I was more than a little tipsy, and, I realised, incredibly comfortable. Once I started to tell her about myself, she'd softened and soon I'd found myself sharing some of my deeper secrets – things I'd only told my closest friends. She had a knack for disarming me with her candour, and matching my confessions with ones that seemed equally intimate. I knew she hadn't been a particularly happy child but loved her life now; that her favourite position was missionary 'but not because it's traditional – just because I like to be fucked'; and that she'd experimented with a variety of kinks. The evening seemed to be heading in one very obvious direction, so I was surprised when she glanced at her watch and said, 'Shit, it's late, I'd better be getting to bed,' and made it clear with her body language that she meant 'alone'. I was on the back foot once again.

"Err, thanks for the drinks," I said.

"You can ask for my number if you want," she replied. "I might even answer your calls."

I felt like a naughty schoolboy for not asking before. "Err, thanks, yes, I'd love it. Let's do dinner sometime." I cringed as the phrase popped out of my mouth by habit.

"Well, if dinner's all you had in mind..." she said, pushing a card into my hand and me out of the door in one move, with a brusque but strangely sensual peck on the cheek. I only realised as I glanced down at the card that she'd never told me her name. It read simply 'Angel'.

I don't know what perfume she wore but it clung to me even as I arrived home. I couldn't help but stroke myself as I lay in bed, thinking of the evening, and came to a fast and messy orgasm over my chest.

Against my usual nature, I called her the next day. There was no response. I tried to blot her out of my mind, assuming she wasn't that interested – why pursue someone who's not into you? But that evening as I had dinner with 'Mandy', I kept finding my thoughts drawn away from my buxom twenty-year old companion and back to Angel. I thought I smelled her perfume at one point and turned around but couldn't see her, so left Mandy at the table and hurried off 'to the loo' in the hope that Angel might be there. She wasn't but, at the end of the night, I couldn't bring myself to share my bed with Mandy, instead craving nothing more than the chance to call Angel again. The phone rang out but she didn't pick up.

After a week, I was frantic. No matter how many distractions I had, work or women, Angel was there insistently tapping on my thoughts making concentration impossible. I left her message after message, feeling like a stalker but unable to resist the urge. And then it came. A text. Five words.

Tonight. My place. My rules.

I was powerless to resist.

Angel opened the door wearing a tight red silk dress.

"I'm impressed. You're on time."

"Of course," I said, proffering the bottle of wine I'd spent an hour choosing.

"Good choice," she nodded appreciatively, putting it on a side-table. "Come through."

As I walked through the door, I smelled her perfume once more and breathed it in wanting to fill my lungs with her scent. Her buttocks undulated under the flimsy fabric of her dress, and I could have sworn that she was wearing stockings underneath. It took all my willpower not to reach out and grab her but I was sure that it would bring the evening to a rapid close.

Instead of leading me through to the lounge, she headed for a room directly ahead and, as she opened the door, I realised it was her bedroom. Opulent was the only word that could describe it: deep red walls, red ceiling, and a red velvet spread on the bed, the colour only broken up by deep fur rugs on the floor.

"Fake," she said, gesturing at them. "Take a seat."

She perched on the edge of the bed and indicated that I sit on the chaise longue opposite – red, of course. I felt like a teenager as she looked at me, the same glint in her eyes that I'd noticed before. If anything, their colour was even brighter now – emerald and almost other-worldly.

"You want me," she said.

Usually I'd deny it – be turned off at such arrogance – but my repeated phone calls belied any excuse I could have made so I merely nodded.

"Then you can have me. But on my terms. And only if you trust me."

Even though I'd only met her once before, the depth of our conversation had been such that I did trust her – something that surprised me.

"I do."

Clearly she was satisfied that I was telling the truth. "Are you happy to do whatever I say?"

Again, I nodded.

"Good. One last thing before we begin. You can stop me at any moment by saying my name three times but if you use my name like that, everything stops and you'll never see me again, so only say it if you're absolutely certain. Agreed?"

One final nod was all it took to seal my fate.

She started gently, taking my hand and pulling me to the bed. Her lips touched mine softly, and I felt the charge of 'anticipation made real' spark through me. She stayed like that, her lips on mine, breathing my breath and feeding me hers, until I was lost, unable to recall a time when we hadn't been joined in a kiss.

Only then did her tongue delicately snake out and touch my own – just the tip. My cock leapt as if she'd grabbed it. But as I started to deepen the kiss she pulled back. "My rules," she said, before moving her lips back to mine and making the world seem right again.

As her tongue leisurely explored, running over my teeth and tongue, stroking the roof of my mouth, I started to shake. She straddled me and, at the same time, I felt her nails begin to slide gently over my back, starting from the base and moving in circles up my spine. By the time she reached my neck, I was almost crying with pleasure, my cock pressing hard against the seam of my jeans. I was sure she could feel me against her. But the sensation was focused on my lips, the point where the softness of our bodies met, the only point at which she was letting me into her.

Both of her hands were now on my neck, nails scratching harder but still sensually, the pads of her fingers pressing into the base of my skull. She moved away once more and whispered 'Kiss me' before pulling my lips hard onto hers. I kissed her deeply, tongues clashing, teeth biting, lips bruising, my hands moving down to her waist and pulling her body close to mine. She rocked her pelvis against me and could feel the arousal fizzing through my muscles. But, just as I was beginning to fear I'd come from that alone, she pulled away once more.

"Strip for me."

My hands fumbling, I pulled my clothes off, throwing them in a heap next to the bed. I looked at her, hoping to see her flesh but she was still fully clothed.

"Now lie back."

I did as she said, cock twitching in anticipation as she climbed on top of me, pushing her dress up to reveal that I'd been right about the stockings. She leaned over me, her nipples brushing achingly close to my face as she grabbed first my left arm, then my right and secured them to the bed with leather cuffs that had been hidden down the sides of the bed when I first walked in. Shimmying down my body, she repeated the action with my ankles. I was now tethered to the bed, unable to move my limbs more than a couple of inches.

"OK?" she asked as she clambered off me and moved to the head of the bed to tighten the straps.

"Yes," I said, despite my nerves, as I was stretched to my maximum.

"Good." She pulled off her knickers and laid them next to my head on the pillow, close enough for me to smell her arousal, but too far away to taste, then sat astride me once more.

Her long hair brushed against my chest as she wriggled down my body, her hot breath tracing a line down my neck, chest, cock, balls and thighs, then continuing down the rest of my body. She knelt at my feet, just looking at me, then ran a leisurely finger up my thighs and cupped my balls softly in her hands.

"You do realise that I can do whatever I want to you now?" she said, her palms massaging my tightening sac.

My cock bobbed in response before I could articulate one.

"And you like that..." she said, a cruel smile in her voice.

Looking me in the eye, she raised her other hand to her mouth and licked her index finger, slowly and deliberately, then leaned forward to run it, glistening, up the seam of my cock. My pre-cum leaked out onto her finger and she traced her fingertip through it in lazy circular motions before bringing it back to her lips to taste.

"Nice," she said, moving further up my body and straddling my thigh so I could feel her wetness leaking out of her as she repeated the gesture.

And so it continued, her running a finger over my cock, tasting it then running it through my pre-cum once again. I was desperate for more direct stimulation but she continued to tease me, her only concession to add more fingers playing over my fraenulum, and dipping into my arousal. I could feel her grinding against me, so wet that her juices were trickling over my thigh and making my balls sticky. And all the while she looked me in the eye. My bonds meant that I couldn't even arch up to get more pressure and I closed my eyes trying to intensify the stimulation through my mind alone.

"Open your eyes," she said.

I watched her bend over my cock, hair trailing over my

inner thighs. I felt a jolt of arousal course through my shaft as I saw her lips heading for my cock but then, just as I was about to slide into her mouth – she stopped. And, looking me directly in the eye, just breathed over me. I had a moment of hope when she gripped the base of my shaft and aimed me between her lips but – no – she kept her mouth wide open. Now, I could feel the warmth of her mouth around me, but no contact – her breath all that she was giving me.

I groaned and tried to push forward, but was frustrated by my ties. She bobbed her head down, brushing the tip of my cock once against her tonsils so fast it was over before I realised what she was doing, then pulled away entirely.

"Is that what you want?"

"Yes," I moaned, now agonised with my need to come.

"Shame," she said, moving away and opening a drawer next to the bed. I gulped when I saw what she had in her hand – a vibrator – and hoped that she wasn't planning to use it on me. But by now, if that was what it would take to get an orgasm, I'd take it. She must have read my mind.

"Greedy boy. But it's not for you."

She sat astride my face and parted her lips with her fingers, inches away from my mouth.

"It's for me."

I watched enraptured as she set the toy buzzing and slid it inside herself, parting her folds. Her finger rubbed on her clit, so near to me that I could see it swelling. I wanted nothing more than to taste her. As she fucked herself with the toy, she held nothing back. Her juices dripped onto my face and I desperately hoped that some would land on my lips but she seemed to know my deepest desires and rocked back and forth until my cheeks, nose and chin were wet yet somehow my lips remained free of her juices. I could see her moving harder, faster now, clearly approaching orgasm. And then…

"What do you want?" she stopped and pulled back, trailing the wet tip of the toy over my chest.

"Anything," I moaned. "Whatever you want."

"OK. I want to fuck you. But you're not allowed to come."

Christ! But I needed to feel her around me, needed to connect. I nodded.

She slid down to my cock and hovered just above it.

"Are you sure?"

I nodded once more, and felt her lips parting over the head of my cock, her warmth sliding just over the head. She stayed like that, flexing her muscles and looking me in the eye, taunting me.

"Do you want to come?"

"Christ, yes!"

"Well you can't."

And with painful slowness, she slid my entire length deep inside her, gripping me tightly and rocking backwards and forwards. My cock was being massaged by her expert muscles and I'd never felt a woman take me so deeply before. It felt like we were joined in bliss, each pulse of hers being matched by one of my own. There was no way I wanted to hold back.

"I've got to come," I begged.

"Your choice," she said, and I remembered the get-out clause. My balls tightened as I gasped, "Angel, Angel, Angel." And shot inside her in an orgasm so intense that I screamed, every nerve in my body feeding the climax, and every muscle in my body shaking. I lay on the bed breathing heavily, and closed my eyes as I tried to return to reality.

When I opened my eyes, she had gone. The leather handcuffs were still around my wrists and ankles but she'd released the ties that held them to the bed. I undid them and grabbed my clothes, pulling them on rapidly. I wanted to hold her, to thank her. But as I got downstairs, I saw a note pinned to the back of the front door.

"Thanks for a great night. Shame you couldn't hold back enough for the next time. Angel."

And I remembered our agreement. "If you use my name like that, everything stops and you'll never see me again."

I realised I'd made the biggest mistake of my life.

The Silken Web
by Virginia Beech

Valet Clarence froze in terror at the sound of Lady Jessica Cleveland's quiet cough behind him. She had silently entered her dressing room, catching him picking through her lingerie. But why had she returned unexpectedly? She should be taking afternoon tea across the Park with Mrs Herbert, the wealthy New Yorker who had rented the widowed Lady Petersfield's Mayfair residence for the London season, hoping to snare a titled gentleman for her daughter Blanche. He had seen her out the front door of Cleveland House, had helped her into the open phaeton and watched as the high-stepping pair of greys had pulled away into Grosvenor Crescent on the drive to Curzon Street. He had not expected her back at 43 Belgrave Square before six o'clock at the earliest, when she would change for dinner at the Hughendon's. He was caught *in flagrante* masturbating into a pair of *milady's* satin knickers. Immediate dismissal from service was inevitable.

Transfixed with fear, Clarence stood silhouetted in the long dressing room looking-glass. One of her Ladyship's silk stockings was knotted tightly around his rampantly rigid cock and smooth balls, which hung out of his unbuttoned breeches like two ripe plums. A shimmering pair of blue satin lace-trimmed knickers dangled incriminatingly from his hand. So frightened was he, that he forgot to remove his stroking hand from his blood-engorged penis, which had been about to jerk its urgent load of hot semen into the sensuously smooth and shiny folds of her fragrantly perfumed underwear.

Lady Jessica's face loomed at his shoulder in the glass's reflection.

"Not content with stealing my intimate apparel, you also defile it."

His stomach knotted in horror. So she knew he had been taking her lingerie! Visions of a prison cell swam before his eyes. He thought of fleeing the room but, even as the futile thought crossed his mind, Lady Cleveland disabused him of that notion.

"I have locked the door. You cannot escape!" Her voice was a steely whisper. This was not the benign and charitable Lady Cleveland he thought he knew.

Clarence dropped the knickers which had suddenly lost their sensual allure and made an ineffectual attempt to remove the stocking. But he had knotted it too tightly. His blood-swollen phallus stood out like a miniature beacon; a purple-headed protuberance that could not subside gracefully back into his breeches.

"Leave my stocking exactly where it is! Turn around from your narcissistic fantasies in my peer-glass so I can properly admire that 'bouquet' you hold in your hand."

Clarence turned, not daring to look up. The silk tied about his cock and balls floated delicately, wafting in the draught caused by his movement. A shaft of afternoon sunlight shone through the stained glass of the dressing room's Burne Jones window, surreally spotlighting his erection in a fractured rainbow.

"Shall I itemise the garments missing from my wardrobe in the three months since you entered valet service here?" The voice was taunting now.

"Six pairs of stockings, a pink satin camisole and

knicker set, a pair of lace-trimmed oyster-coloured French knickers, a pair of long-sleeved satin opera gloves, the blush pink sateen corset from my Parisian corsetiere Isadora, and a pair of high-heeled button shoes!"

Clarence blanched as Lady Cleveland continued: "I informed you I would be taking tea with Mrs Herbert this afternoon because I knew you were stealing my intimate apparel and I was determined to catch you red-handed. I had Housekeeper search your room this morning while you were at your duties. I am sure you know what she found hidden there."

She contemplated the bleak dismay on the valet's stricken face with gloating satisfaction. Her gaze lowered to admire the spectacle of his exposed balls and still rigid cock neatly tied and held like a bridal nose-gay.

Clarence was speechless as his real and fantasy worlds collapsed in humiliation about him. Having been brought to this new life of opportunity from Madam Blanchette's 'molly house', a discreet male brothel off London's Tottenham Court Road catering to the unusual carnal lusts of the nobility and *nouveau riche* industrialists, all hopes of preferment from personal valet to butler now lay on the silk carpet with her Ladyship's dropped knickers. Prison gates beckoned.

"Pick them up!" Lady Cleveland hissed. "I will not allow my undergarments to touch the floor, though I shall not wear those again now that you have defiled them with that excrescence protruding so obscenely from your breeches."

Clarence hastened to retrieve the satin knickers from the carpet and stood with head bowed, his hands ineffectually attempting to hide his exposed pecker. The swollen appendage was beginning to throb painfully from the tight knotting. Its head was now a deep blood-engorged shade; a pulsating purple mushroom that would wait in vain to be stroked to its fruitful outcum.

"Divest yourself of your uniform and show me that infamously pretty body and anal garden of delight you have prostituted so often for the carnal pleasure of my reprobate husband and his degenerate cronies at Madam Blanchette's before I bought you from her."

Clarence looked up to meet Lady Jessica's gaze, not believing he had heard correctly. He gasped in disbelief! She was no longer wearing her afternoon tea dress. She stood there, a statuesque apparition in a form-fitting black sateen corset, its restrictive lace-up accentuating the curvaceous contours of her hourglass figure and full breasts. A hand rested imperiously upon the swell of her hip. She wore no knickers and his shocked eyes were drawn to her smoothly shaved pussy provocatively framed by the curved rim of her shiny corset and its taut suspender straps holding her stockings to her thighs.

Her piercing blue eyes bored into him like an angry cobra that hypnotises its prey before striking.

"Obey me this instant! Or I shall have you inside Newgate prison before the sun goes down."

Clarence moved with alacrity at this tiniest hint of reprieve. Within a trice he had discarded his valet uniform; the white cotton shirt, hunter-green velveteen breeches buckled below the knee, matching hose and silver buckled pumps. Would he ever wear the Cleveland Household uniform again?

Clarence was not to know it, but Lady Jessica knew more about him than she would ever admit. The Clevelands owned a swathe of property in North London, including Madam Blanchette's infamous establishment of rent boys. It had been a simple matter to pressure the bawd to part with a suitably attractive boy for her intended particular esoteric pleasures. Madam Blanchette had assured her, as she gratefully pocketed a handsome purse of guineas, that

Clarence would suit her purposes nicely. His proclivity for sexual fantasy and pleasure in cross-dressing for the brothel's distinguished patrons, marked him as the perfect choice for restrictive training and sissy grooming.

She had monitored her quarry's popularity as a rent boy for some months before persuading Madam Blanchette to part with him. His physique and Adonine looks had been much in demand. His sweetcheeks and the hidden flower that nestled between them were the object of desire for everyone who gathered to play Baccarat there on Wednesday evenings. Her rich clientele would play for high stakes to win his body, the jackpot prize offered at the conclusion of the evening's play. Blanchette would lead Clarence through the blue haze of Havana cigar smoke into the gaming room. He would be presented naked but for a pair of her silk knickers which she had wet down to cling to his youthful buttocks in near transparent sensuality.

The delighted winner would rise to claim his prize. To expectant hush, he would pull the clinging garment down to expose Clarence's wetly glistening and pertly rounded cheeks, dangling twin jewels and long penis with its turned-up knob that awaited the caress of milking hand or lusting lips to arouse it. The rampantly excited squire would lead Clarence to a large ottoman to debauch him before the assembled players.

Some winners buggered 'rough'. General Chalmondeslay, lately returned from India where he had earned the sobriquet of "Leatherdick" in the barrack rooms of the Bengal Lancers, would bend Clarence brusquely over, parting his buttocks to expose the target of attack. Without bothering to reconnoitre the terrain, he would cry "Huzzah!". Taking his 'lance' in hand would advance unchecked into the valley of the undefended opening splayed invitingly before his lustful gaze. His frenzied onslaught would culminate in a copious discharge before he withdrew from the fray.

Lord Cleveland on the other hand, (so Lady Jessica's informant had whispered), preferred a more leisurely frontal congress; enjoying the feel of Clarence's lithe warm body while creaming his butthole with a languorous rhythm before going down to suck his cock to creamy cum.

Lady Jessica also knew about Clarence's regular 'specials'; robed as the Abbess to cane the bared buttocks of the Bishop of Yarmouth when he was in town; dressed up as schoolgirl Doris for an OTK spanking by Judge Trevose. She was aware also of Clarence's penchant for dressing up in Blanchette's own lace-up corsets and billowing petticoats to receive a noble buttfuck. And he was not averse to assuaging Blanchette's own demanding clitoral urges on those frequent occasions when a jaded client required visual titillation before creaming his glory gape.

The long awaited moment had come for Lady Jessica Cleveland to discard her blushing English Rose image and emerge as the Domina that had always slumbered within her breast. She would transform Clarence into the submissive Slutmaid she had secretly desired for her personal boudoir slave. He would be the felicitous foil to her hitherto suppressed sensuality.

Knowing his latent transvestite desires, she had arranged to leave temptation open for him to steal her intimate apparel. It had taken just three months to ensnare the fly in her silken web.

"Here are my garments that Housekeeper found in your room. Since you so obviously enjoy wearing them, you will entertain me by donning them now."

Clarence could not believe his ears or eyes. His head swam. He watched in fascinated awe as she unpinned and shook the mass of silver locks to cascade aver her shoulders and the proud expanse of her corseted breasts. Was this really Lady Cleveland? Were his most secret sexual fantasies about to be played out in her private dressing room before her gaze?

He had worshipped this haughty, silver-haired lady ever since she had spirited him away from Madam Blanchette's to a new life at Cleveland House in elegant Belgravia. It had been his secret pleasure to surreptitiously 'borrow' her lingerie when it was sent down to the laundry in the basement, or take it directly from her closet when she was out. At end of the day he would retire to his top-floor room, undress and luxuriate in the joy of donning her silks and satins before stroking himself to orgasm.

Just stepping into her knickers and slithery camisole slip, drawing the silk stockings up over his shapely legs and savouring the erotic feel of silk running up the tender inside of his thighs would bring his cock to throbbing erection. He would stand before his peer-glass; a Hermaphroditus regarding his reflection in the pool of Salmacis as he ran his satin-gloved hands over his corseted body, fondling the sensitive glans of his prick through the slinky quicksilver perfection of Lady Jessica's satin knickers. He liked to tie his erect penis and plump balls in her silk stocking, enjoying the pressure of the blood pumping through the veins of his distended shaft as he stroked and fondled himself to explosive release, fantasising that it was the statuesque Mistress of the House who stood there pleasuring herself *en dishabille*.

How he had yearned to possess such a curvaceously feminine body. Filled with breast envy, he would squeeze his own tiny tits and pretend they were her full breasts and firm nipples that he had freed from the prison of her figure-hugging corset to admire, hold and suck.

Sometimes he slid her knickers down to his knees and stood before the peer-glass, his stockinged legs wide apart to hold the knickers taut. Then he would whip his own buttocks in a frenzy of self-flagellation with his leather belt, enjoying the reflection of his white cheeks blushing pink to red to purple in painful progression before cockstroking himself to ecstasy.

Lady Cleveland broke into his reverie. "Hurry up! I do not intend to stand here all day while you day-dream."

Clarence pulled himself together and took the bundle of clothes over to the *chaise-longue* against the wall and sat down. His submissive fantasies had suddenly taken on a true dimension over which he had absolutely no control. He didn't know where she was leading him but it wasn't on a one-way trip to Newgate!

Clarence thankfully undid the constraining stocking around his balls and prick, aching now from their prolonged constriction. Picking out the white satin knickers trimmed with lace, he stepped delicately into them. They barely covered his posterior, showing an excess of youthful white cheeks while his balls and cock thrust out in bulging relief through the shiny material.

Picking up the sateen corset, he put it back to front around his stomach, did up its ten hooks and pulled it round so that they were at the back. Its tight whale-boned constriction brought a tingle of excitement to his abdomen and his cock rose in tumescent excitement.

There was a glint of approval in Lady Jessica's eyes at the practised dexterity with which Clarence fitted the body shaping garment to his frame. Madame Blanchette had had a willing cross-dresser to entertain admirers.

Clarence drew the flimsy, gossamer-thin lace-topped hose slowly up over his long legs and snapped the corset's suspender tabs to the stocking tops, pulling them sleekly taut against his thighs. He could not resist running his hands down his sides to feel the hour-glass femininity of the corsetry now moulding his figure, and enjoy the luxurious thrill of sensuality that always overcame him at such a moment of bodily restriction. He slipped his feet into the high-heeled bootees. Next, Clarence picked up the white satin French slip. He slid into it, drawing it sensuously up over his body, engaging in the erotic quicksilver feel of the material slithering over his stockinged legs and thighs to cover his nipples. Finally, he eased his hands into the elbow-length pink satin gloves to complete the erotic picture of himself in the glass.

Lady Cleveland turned to a hatbox on her vanity table and drew out a thickly curled blonde wig. Clarence's eyes lit up as she handed it to him; the crowning glory to this unexpected and unexplained enforced feminine make-over at her hands.

Clarence regarded himself in the long vanity glass. But for the lack of rounded bosom to fill the slip, the feminine transformation was complete. A sensually beautiful, blonde, young woman in slinky satin lingerie gazed dreamily back at him. The sight, and the unaccustomed situation was disturbingly exciting and his cock throbbed in constricted excitement within its tight satin confines. He knew that Lady Cleveland could see the thrusting bulge of his cock beneath the satin slip and feared he might spontaneously cum at the sheer stunning pleasure of wearing such fragrantly perfumed lingerie in the presence of this statuesque, corseted lady.

Lady Jessica moved to his side with the catlike fluidity of a stalking predator to break into his reverie of erotic fantasy. Her voice was a velvet feline purr.

"Do you enjoy sheathing your pretty body in my silks and satins? Do you love my knickers' satin caress against your throbbing prick? Is this how you jerk off in your room? Do you watch yourself stroking your hot pussycock with that satin-gloved hand? Shall I watch you stain my tight knickers with your spurting cream? Will you cum in front of me now?"

Clarence's hand went to his cock to stroke its throbbing heat through its satin confines. A wet patch of pre-cum spread its telltale message of imminent orgasm.

Lady Jessica's voice cut like a whiplash into the sexual fantasy she had conjured up.

"I shall punish you for your outrageous presumption and theft of my intimate belongings and you will accept my punishment without reservation."

A shocked Clarence came crashing down to earth and reality. Tears welled up in his eyes as he knelt in supplication before his Mistress.

"I beg you not to send me to Newgate, my Lady. I will do anything to serve as your adoring boudoir maid. I shall worship you as your abject slave if you will keep me. Have pity on me."

It was unconditional surrender; a moment that Lady Jessica had been preparing for ever since she had collected Clarence from Madam Blanchette's. Her firm measured voice now held a note of triumph.

"You will henceforward answer to the name of Clarissa and none other. You will address me when I speak to you as 'Mistress'. Lord Cleveland will no longer use you as his personal valet. He will forget you existed after today. He prefers to dip his quill into a 'Bit o' Rough' at Blanchette's, not the feminised sissy I intend to make of you!

"I shall confine you to my suite while I groom you for your transformation and new role as my personal boudoir Slutmaid. While I whip you into shape, I shall teach you all my preferences and whims in dress, toilette and punishment rituals of disciplined sensuality. Do I make myself clear?"

"Yes, Mistress!"

"You will learn to bare and present your bottom in my preferred punishment posture. I shall discipline you daily, taking a whippy cane to your bottom and a leather strap to your pussycock as part of your behaviour modification. I shall depilate every hair of your body except your eyelashes, submit you to a regular body massage and diet that will soften your body curves, encourage your breasts and bottom to blossom into the rounded femininity that you desire and I require for my pleasure."

Taking a leather collar and leash from a drawer, she slipped it around his neck and fastened it.

"You now wear my training collar and I shall leash you while I teach you feminine deportment and Slutmaid servility. I shall enclose your pussycock in a leather chastity harness which you will wear at all times unless I remove it for my personal pleasure. You will cum when and where I wish and on no other occasion, on pain of my cane.

"When I am sufficiently satisfied with your progress, I shall fit you with a custom made collar of hammered gold which can never be removed. You must accept me as your Dominatrix and my terms of lifelong service now, or be delivered to the police for theft. Which is it to be?"

Clarence bent forward and kissed the toe of her proffered booted foot with reverence.

"I accept my fate at your gracious hands in humble gratitude, Mistress."

Jessica smiled with satisfaction.

"Now you wear my collar, there can be no turning back. Your previous existence must be forgotten history. No more buttfucks from noble cocks! Clarence is dead. You are now Clarissa. You belong to me. You are my personal property, my toygirl, my private *divertissement* for boudoir, bed and bath. Your slutmaidenly sweetcheeks, fuckbutton and pussycock belong exclusively to me. You are my personal plaything, my pleasure toy!"

Clarence listened to Mistress's words with fear that turned to mounting joy as the future of his transformation and submission became clear. Fantasy had become fact. He gulped, choking back tears of pent-up emotion. He took a deep breath, closed his eyes and mentally stepped through the Looking-glass; an Alice entering a promised Wonderland.

"I am Clarissa. You are my Mistress, my Goddess. I place myself in your hands in loving submission. I pledge you my unquestioning obedience in everything. I shall serve you as your Slutmaid with my body and my soul in total adoration.

I am now your life commitment, Clarissa. Your Domina! Your sun and your moon! I am the Alpha and Omega of your existence! In return for your total submission to me, I promise to care for you and your every need for the rest of my life."

Jessica stood, legs apart, an awesome demanding Dominatrix. She put a hand to her smoothly shaved cunt and parted the pink lips.

"Worship now, at the altar of your Goddess!"

There was a moment of silence. With a moan of pleasure Clarissa buried her face in Jessica's hot cunt. Nuzzling deep in ecstatic adoration, she sucked at the precious jewel she found there, coaxing it from its protective hood into prominent arousal. Then, darting her tongue into the musky recesses of the bower, she sipped at her Domina's sacred cup of life.

The ormolu clock on the wall whirred and pinged out the hour as Clarissa made the ultimate submission. It was 4 o'clock!

At that moment Lady Cleveland and valet Clarence died. Domina Jessica and Slutmaid Clarissa were born.

Lot Twenty-One
by Andrea Carver

I never expected to be allowed in to this exclusive men's club. It was hard to believe such places still existed. Dinner jackets, leather armchairs, and the air – fuggy with cigar smoke and the scent of fine alcohol – surely belonged to a different era.

I was here because I'd organised a charity auction for a cause close to my heart, and I was determined to raise as much money as possible, but as I looked around at the hundred or so company directors, stock market millionaires and aristocrats, I began to appreciate the sheer wealth in the room. The twenty lots I had secured as prizes now seemed tired and ordinary – these men could buy a hot-air balloon trip with the change in their pockets. I realised what we needed was something to grab their interest, something that didn't come up for auction very often, if ever. That's when I decided to put myself up as an additional lot – Lot twenty-one.

A bit *Pretty Baby* I know, but my motives were not entirely selfless. As well as raising money for a cause I believed in, I was seizing the chance to fulfil a favourite fantasy, which always began with me being purchased.

It's widely believed that some fantasies should remain just that, but as the auction proceeded through the lots, so the arousal built up inside me. I was really going through with this. I was going to be purchased!

I was nervous too. Would anyone bid for Lot twenty-one? Would they be scandalised? Could I be arrested for what I was offering?

The auctioneer, Adrian – my friend, confidant and accomplice – had assured me that a private gentlemen's club meant just that. The auction would take place behind closed doors; deeds done within the confines of the building would go no further, and I would *definitely* be well received.

When Adrian announced the additional item and presented me as Lot twenty-one, a ripple of anticipation went through the room. At twenty-five, I was half the age of the youngest men gathered before me and the evening dress I'd chosen displayed my body beautifully, my nipples presenting themselves prominently under the blue silk. I could almost hear the men salivating, feel them undressing me, mentally fucking me already.

'Gentlemen, to clarify: you will be bidding for access to a place as yet unexplored by man – the final place this young lady remains a virgin.' Adrian turned me around and stroked a hand over my buttocks to emphasise the offer. 'Tonight this virginity is to be willingly surrendered to the successful bidder of Lot twenty-one.'

The murmurs grew to a roar.

Adrian had assured me this would be a popular lot. Anal sex was a common male fantasy, he'd said. True, they could pay a hooker a lot less than they'd pay tonight, but it was also a common fantasy to have a virgin. I was offering both.

I'd left the stage before the bidding began, and now waited nervously in a heavy-Victorian style bedroom upstairs.

I knew it was bad news to be so tense – I didn't want to make myself impenetrable – but I couldn't help it. Every time my eyes caught sight of the pretty china bowl on the bedside table, which had been filled with a selection of lubricants in preparation, the butterflies began. What the hell was I doing? Adrian had promised to steer the bidding in favour of a younger man, but what if he couldn't? What if I ended up with some hoary old goat? The reality of what I was doing caught up with me. Perhaps this hadn't been such a good idea after all. Perhaps it should have remained a fantasy.

When the knock came I opened the door with shaking hands and was relieved to find a rather attractive gentleman standing on the threshold. Not quite six foot, trim, with light blue eyes and well-cut silver hair. I put him in his early sixties.

He smiled a lovely smile – a gentleman's smile, and handed me a receipt bearing Adrian's signature – proof the man standing before me had been the highest bidder at…

How much?

I gulped. I hoped I'd be worth it.

We started off with reassurances. Yes, I was sure. Yes, he knew what he was doing, and would be very gentle with me. Then he poured the drinks – champagne – all the time talking to me in a wonderful, soft, cultured voice that put me at ease.

He told me his wife wouldn't even discuss anal, and that he'd paid call-girls on a few occasions to satisfy his desire. He'd been determined to win me – more so when the bidding had culminated in a war between himself and an old rival who, on description, sounded like the very hoary old goat I'd feared. He couldn't possibly have allowed *that* one loose on such a beautiful young woman, he said. Gratitude towards this man overwhelmed me, giving me confidence to begin.

His eyes widened with delight as I slipped off my dress, revealing a virginal white lace basque and stockings. I had shaved my pussy, hoping to emphasise my innocence in this particular sexual activity, but my nipples stood proud and whore-red above the lace of the cups.

He gave a quick glance at my face and then the gap between us closed. His mouth sucked hungrily on my nipple, tongue teasing, teeth grazing, while the other was rolled, thumbed and pinched so hard it was difficult to distinguish between pain and pleasure.

Appreciative noises came from deep in his throat as a well-manicured hand left my breast to run up my leg, encountering bare flesh above the stocking tops. Warm breath heated my neck as he murmured his intention to make this enjoyable for me. He turned me around to face away from him. Thoroughly aroused, I wriggled my arse against him in encouragement.

His hands came around my front, pulling down the cups of the basque. My breasts fell heavily into his warm palms, my nipples growing harder and longer as he took them between his thumbs and forefingers, continuing the rolling, pinching, sending electric pulses down between my legs until I arched my back and pushed my arse back into his crotch, feeling his clothed cock squeezing in between my cheeks.

He would allow me to do nothing. When my hand went behind in search of his fly, it was moved away, and instead I was bent forward, gently, over a bolster on the bed.

I parted my legs, keeping them locked straight, putting my pussy high on display, where it glistened, I knew. I wished this encounter was for conventional sex. He'd aroused me. I was craving to be filled, but *my* needs were not what he'd bid for, and even this thought excited me. He'd bought me, and soon he would possess me.

Large, warm hands caressed my buttocks, and I raised them even higher, extending my invitation. He parted my cheeks, opening them, exposing me to cold air until his breath warmed my most private place as he kissed me.

'My beautiful rose,' he whispered, sending nervous thrills through me. Yes it's yours, I thought. Just for tonight, you own it. It's yours for the taking.

His fingers spread my pussy juices back and over my hole and then he chose a tube from the bowl. I felt warm jelly wetting my entrance, the pad of a finger pressing gently as he spread the lubricant until I was fabulously slippery and the finger entered, slowly, carefully.

Even this made me gasp. Being entered for the first time sent my muscles clenching around the invading finger. He bent close to my ear, whispering coaxing words, telling me how beautiful I was, how perfect my arse felt, how he hoped to give me pleasure as well.

A second finger was introduced, bringing more warm, slippery lube with it, preparing me. I was aroused, wet, receptive – unexpectedly desperate for him to fill me with something more substantial than the fingers sliding in and out, in and out.

I gave a groan that said I was ready. His fingers withdrew. Hands parted my buttocks again, opening them even wider until I thought I would split, then the tip of his cock was nudging my last frontier.

My muscles tightened instinctively, and again his soft, coaxing voice caressed my ears so that I focused on relaxing for him.

He reached my ring, which was tight and unyielding. I was dismayed, but his excitement increased as he manoeuvred his cock against the barrier in such an expert manner, I was assured he really did know what he was doing. Guttural grunts escaped him as he worked at my ring, pressing forward until he was able to prise me open.

The tip slipped through then, quite suddenly, piercing me. I cried out. It hurt.

He'd behaved like such a gentleman so far, I was half

expecting an apology for my pain. Instead, he growled how wonderfully tight I was around his cock, that he was now going to open me up, and oh, how my narrow little passage was going to milk him.

I realised then, however gentle, kind and polite he might be, my cry as he'd broken through had been the highlight of this coupling for him. This was what it was all about; this is what he'd paid for – the sounds of a virgin being taken. He'd paid to hear my discomfort as he forced his way up my arse.

My eyes were watering. The pressure of his cock seemed to fill my whole existence. I was aware of nothing else. I pressed my face into the bed and clutched at the bedcovers as he pushed further in, stretching my narrow passage more than was surely possible. His cock felt enormous as it invaded my very core, filling my belly with throbbing muscle. My cries were genuine, and I did nothing to hold them back, knowing it was what he wanted to hear. My distress was his excitement. It was more than I could take I was sure, and was about to tell him so, when he withdrew a little, pushed back in, withdrew some more, pushed back in.

The lube was spreading, easing his path. His cock began to slide smoothly, and was beginning to be tolerable until, like the nipple-pinching, it became difficult to distinguish between pain and pleasure.

He stopped, presumably to allow me to get used to his presence.

'No, go on,' I pleaded, desperate now, as a climax began to stir – not from his actions, but from the excitement of fulfilling my fantasy – allowing a stranger to buy me and take me in the arse.

I pushed back, plunging him in up to the hilt which made us both shout – him with surprise, me with the shock of just how far he'd penetrated. Immediately he grasped my hips and, with my encouragement, began thrusting harder, his balls smacking against my very wet, bare pussy. This was now desperate – for both of us. Any nervousness on my part or gentleness on his had flown as he fucked me with animal need, and I wanted it. I wanted it so badly. Fingers slipped round and spread my lips, and I cried out, my clit so hard and high it was almost unbearable to have him touch it.

Instantly I was coming; coming hard and loud.

A few remorseless thrusts deep, deep in my belly and he gave a bestial groan. I felt his cock spasm violently against my walls and then he emptied himself into me, flooding my arse with hot cum, heating my insides, and it felt so, so good.

My muscles, now at least doing something familiar, helped evacuate him from my body and we collapsed, panting and gasping onto the bed, my plundered arse on fire from its first fuck.

He pulled me to him. I was held, kissed, told I was the most amazing woman, and thanked for giving him the privilege of taking my anal virginity.

He was a gentleman through and through, and I couldn't have wished for a better person to win that bid. He'd made it a wonderful, surprisingly exciting experience. The charity would receive more money than we could ever have anticipated, and I had fulfilled a fantasy, all thanks to Lot twenty-one.

Public Exposure
by Cathryn Cooper

Here she was wearing nothing but shoes, a pair of sheer chocolate-coloured stockings and a waist-nipping pink corset trimmed with coffee-coloured lace. The tight fitting corset finished just under her breastbone leaving her bosoms exposed and thrusting forwards like ripe grapefruit. The whole ensemble was hidden by the sensual soft luxury of a cashmere coat lined with silk. The silk was cool and more sensual than the cashmere, caressing as it did her naked flesh.

Valentine, an on/off, overly handsome, overly sexed acquaintance from way back, had told her she was clothes obsessed and that it was a wonder she didn't open a shop.

'That's exactly what I want to do,' she said to him. 'And I would if I had the money.'

And so he'd suggested a series of dares. They would all start at a pre-arranged place, and all end at a pre-arranged place. This week it was the shopping centre.

Her four inch heels clicked confidently along the pavement.

'Tell me what sensations you're feeling,' he said to her.

She smiled. Valentine was under the distinct impression that this scenario was entirely of his making. She'd let him think that, and as he imagined her nakedness beneath the cashmere coat, she considered the stirrings in his loins, the lengthening of his penis.

Mallory sighed and a slight smile curved the corners of her mouth. She didn't particularly want to say anything at all. What she was doing, what was happening to her was something solitary, for her alone to enjoy. On the other hand Valentine couldn't help be aroused by the thought of her semi-naked body.

'It's wonderful,' she said as they skirted a policeman who at that moment was engrossed in directing two lost tourists.

'We're in a public place,' she murmured. 'What can I say?'

Sliding Valentine a sidelong look, she was in time to see him swallow hard. The poor man must be going through purgatory; look but don't touch; not yet, not here walking down a main street at midday.

'Well,' he said, gulping down a low groan. 'Tell me how it feels. Not in any great detail. Not erotically. Just...'

She turned up the collar of the coat. The day was chill and a hint of snow, or at least an overnight frost, tingled in the air.

'I'm tingling,' she whispered. 'My flesh is tingling at the thrill of this. My sex is covered in goose bumps. I've shaved it. It's hot in the middle but chilly on the outside. Can you imagine that? I know you haven't seen it yet, but at least you can IMAGINE how it looks – denuded – vulnerable – at the mercy of the winter chill.' Her voice was provocative, yet hushed and as soft as the silk lining that caressed her naked body and teased her senses.

The truth was that her shaved crotch wasn't really that cold at all. Her sex was tantalised and burned between her legs.

'Describe it to me,' he said. 'I demand that you describe it to me.'

Ah! There it was. The macho domination was beginning

to show. He did not raise his voice. He did not look at her. 'Go on. Now,' he demanded.

'I'm trying to think. I need the right words.' She smiled to herself. The truth was that she was determined to take her time, enjoy what she was experiencing. It wasn't just about the fact that she was wearing so little beneath the coat. It was the fact that she was doing it in public. The world whirled around her; futures traders with pink faces and loose ties, lean-hipped office juniors with pinched cheeks and boot black eyes, mothers in dirndl skirts and crepe-soled boots, old people wearing thick scarves and hats that covered their ears. What would they do, she wondered, if suddenly she whipped her coat off and flashed them her very best assets.

She took a deep breath and thought about how she felt. Not just with regard to her nakedness beneath the swishing coat. That was only something to be relished like thick cream on coffee cake. This was something she hadn't expected, and was incomparable to anything she'd ever done before. She liked it enough to forget that he was walking at her side, yet she could not.

Valentine had presence. He had dark good looks, black hair that curled untidily over his collar, black eyes that seemed to look into her very soul. His body was lean but muscular. He was handsome in a brooding, dramatic kind of way. He drew admiring looks. Even now, secretaries bustling by on lunch-time breaks glanced in his direction.

'You still haven't answered,' he said to her. 'Tell me how you feel. Give me just a few words. Give me just one word.'

'Erotic.'

It was the first word that came to mind. How else could she describe what she was doing, what she was thinking?

Delicious shivers of excitement and sensual pleasure made her nipples harden and become almost painful with their need for release. Wetness oozed from the warm lips that nestled provocatively between her silky soft thighs.

'Very erotic. Arousing!'

She stressed the words. Beneath the coat her hips swayed as she tried to elicit the last ounce of sexual turn-on from the cool silk lining. She trembled, and her inhibitions flew away.

'That's not a very good description,' he grumbled. 'I think you could do better. And you haven't really put yourself out that much. You're not exposed to any great extent. Not really. But you will be soon. I guarantee it.'

The last sentences were as much a threat as a promise. He would teach her to keep him waiting.

Tossing her hair, she eyed him sidelong with catlike wickedness. The soft darkness of her lashes briefly alighted on her creamy cheeks. Her dark pink lips widened into a smile.

'If you dare.'

'I dare,' he said, his eyes narrowing.

She shivered. What did he have in store for her?

Beneath the impenetrable barrier of her coat, her nipples erected against the silk lining, her buttocks quivering as though caressed by the fingertips of an unseen lover. She buried her hands more deeply in her pockets and nestled her chin down into the collar.

The brightly lit shops and offices were left behind. The street narrowed. They turned off into another street of boarded up shops; old shops with deep doorways and windows sealed with metal shutters or wood.

'In here,' he said, tugging her off balance and into one of the doorways. 'Now,' he said, his hands resting on either side of her head. 'Undo your buttons.'

She glanced over his shoulder. There were fewer people passing by on this street, but it was far from empty.

'Now,' he said impatiently.

With trembling fingers, she did as he asked undoing the top button, then the next, then the next…Within her body that bud of passion that sat so secretly between lips of pink flesh was reminding her of its existence, reminding her of the effect her lurid thoughts could have on it. Fleetingly, she glanced at the other people hurrying along the pavement. As he opened the front of her coat, she voiced what was in her mind.

'What if someone sees me?'

His smile was wide enough to cut his face in half. 'That's the whole point. It's the danger of being found out. My body's between you and them. You have to give into my body in order to be shielded from prying eyes. Exciting, don't you think?'

Her body bristled with anticipation as draughts of cool air caressed her slim thighs but did nothing to cool the heat that burned between her legs.

'They see nothing. They hear nothing. But they might,' he added. 'They just might.'

For a moment he feasted his eyes on her nakedness, holding the coat open so that she was exposed to the cold air. She shivered. Her nipples were like frozen lead, sticking outwards and forwards, aching for something more to happen.

'You look glorious,' he said. 'Undo me. Get me out and put me into you.'

She did as he requested, unzipping his trousers, fumbling into his underwear to extricate his cock. Obediently she opened her legs and despite their exposed situation, she moaned as she rubbed the velvet soft head along her slick furrow.

Once he was inside her, he pinned her back against the metal shutter protecting the door, his fingers tightly gripping her wrists. Lowering his mouth, he licked at each bosom in turn.

At the same time, he thrust himself more forcefully into her, so forcefully that she had to stand on tiptoe as he lifted her off the floor.

She closed her eyes trying not to see the passers by, feeling exposed, feeling that she had no choice in this. She was helpless and ashamed to say, was enjoying the experience.

His tongue followed the contours of her breasts, tracing each gentle curve and valley; his tongue lapped her satin flesh, around the dark halos in which her nipples sat demanding and receiving avid attention.

She thrust her hips towards his, inviting him to thrust more, lost in the moment and no longer caring whether anyone saw what they were doing.

She closed her eyes in order to better savour the sensations. She shifted slightly and opened her legs a little wider. Leg and thigh muscles trembling, she arched her body towards him. Gradually her surroundings faded into nothing. She was lost in her own delirium as he pounded into her, arousing sensations she never knew existed.

Falling more deeply into the abyss of her own sexuality, Mallory didn't care when Valentine pushed her coat further off her shoulders. If anyone had peered in they would have seen her state of undress. But she didn't care. Valentine's cock was seducing her clitoris, tempting it out, tingling it, rubbing it, bringing it closer and closer to orgasm.

'You dirty bitch,' she heard him say. 'You're enjoying this. You'd enjoy it if someone was watching. You'd enjoy it if I offered you to one of the greasy mechanics or a pimply-faced office clerk. You'd take it. You'd take mine in the front, one in the mouth and one in the arse. Wouldn't you, you dirty bitch! Wouldn't you!'

His voice sounded distant and she gave no response. She was lost in her own pleasure, her legs taut as she tilted her hips to meet his, her vulva swirling with liquid desire.

Tingles of pleasure spread upwards and outwards.

She squealed as he let go her hands and pushed the coat down her arms. It fell to the floor. She gasped. 'But everyone…'

'Bend over.'

One hand on her neck, one on her waist, he turned her around to she was facing the metal screen. He pushed her head down, his hand pressing on her neck. She stared at the coat lying on the ground, thought about protesting that she was getting goose bumps, but knew it wouldn't do any good.

'Brace yourself,' he said.

It was as though what he wanted, or perhaps her own desire lying deep inside, but she did as he said, bracing her palms against the cold metal shutter. She felt him nudging her buttocks apart. The slippery head of his cock slid up and down her crack, like a snake seeking the way into a favourite lair.

'The ultimate exposure,' she heard him say.

Her head met the metal shutter as he pushed into her sacred hole. This was something she had done before, but never in these circumstances. Just as he had said, this was the ultimate exposure.

She could tell by the sounds he was making that he wouldn't be long. No! That wouldn't be fair.

'What…about…me?'

His thrusts were hard now. She could only get out one word at a time. Her breasts swung backwards and forwards with each powerful shove.

Without a word, he brought one hand around to cup her left breast whilst the fingers of his right hand dived between her legs.

'That's it!' she moaned.

It was as though an orgasm had exploded from the tips of his fingers. Every fibre of her being jolted with the intensity of it. Her legs shook.

'That's what I like! I love to have you come. You coming makes me come…'

His voice broke off into an anguished growl as he stiffened and filled her with his essence, so much essence that some escaped and ran down her legs like weak icing.

'Same time next week?' said Mallory once she was properly – or rather, improperly dressed.

'Of course.'

Her phone rang two minutes after she got back to her flat. It was Stephen, her boyfriend.

'How was it?' she said.

'The guys loved it. They all paid up without a murmur. You'll have enough money to open that shop before you know it. Same time next week?'

'You bet. That's the lease deposit taken care of. Now for the stock.'

Personal Shopper
by Izzy French

Will he, won't he,' Christina wondered as the man paced across the front of the shop for the tenth type. She hoped he would. A tall, dark and handsome cliché. She wondered who was his lucky significant other. Wife, girlfriend, lover? He did a ninety-degree turn and pushed the door open. At last, thought Christina. The glance she gave Kate, her assistant, said, 'He's mine.' As proprietor of Whispers and Promises, Christina could pick and choose which customers she served. There had to be some perks. And it had been a slow day. Christina had been bored, if she was honest. And customers needed nurturing, didn't they?

"Hi, how may I help?" she asked, smoothing her skirt down and smiling.

"I'm looking for some underwear. A nice set. It's for her birthday."

"Her?"

"Yes."

The non-committal type, Christina thought.

"What size is she?"

"Size 10. 34C." Christina could feel his eyes rove over her, probably assessing her figure against that of the woman he was buying for. She felt a tingle of pleasure. How did she compare? Well, she hoped. Her shiny black hair was tied back, emphasising her high cheekbones and glossy red lips, and her black skirt and white blouse hugged her breasts, waist, hips. She was a good advert for the shop, she felt confident of that.

"Same as me," she smiled. "I'll get some sets together and you can see what you think would suit her." She whipped around the shop, quickly returning to the counter, arms full of lace and silk.

"There you go. Must be so hard to choose for someone else. If she was here I'd suggest she tried them on, of course." Christina nodded her head towards the changing rooms at the back of the shop.

When she glanced back again he was staring at her intently. His eyes were dark, unreadable. She held his gaze for a few moments, then looked away and began pulling together sets of French knickers and balconette bras in black, crimson, cool ivory. The silk slipped between her fingers, she tussled with the thin straps, her fingers trembling slightly as she sensed him watching each tiny movement. Kate was busying herself with folding an untidy pile of pretty camisoles. Christina felt alone with this man. It was almost 5pm, a quiet time of the day. People rushed by outside, not even glancing in, anxious to get home.

"I like that, and this one too," he said, his hand brushing against hers as he pulled two bras from the pile, one black, the other purple. He examined each carefully, brushing the fabric with his fingers.

"Beautiful, aren't they? Designed to be taken off."

Christina had sensed his fingers rested on hers just slightly longer than was necessary.

"There are French knickers or thongs to match either," she said. "Which would you prefer?"

"French knickers, I'm kind of old fashioned." This was the first time he smiled. It reached his eyes.

"I'm with you on that. Thongs leave little to the imagination. Something more romantic, and more comfortable about French knickers." Christina returned his smile.

"Let me match them up then you can decide which you'd like to take. We offer a gift wrapping service too." Christina found the matching French knickers, brushed everything else to one side and laid both sets carefully alongside each other on the glass-topped counter. They were both exquisite, made of silk, trimmed with lace, the bras under-wired. The black one had a glossy, satin sheen, the purple one a matt finish. Either was guaranteed to make a woman look and feel great, Christina had chosen her stock with care.

"I'd like to see them on." His voice was quiet, but authoritative.

"But she's not with you."

"No, I want you to try them on for me." His tone was insistent.

Christina hesitated, looked down at the slips of silk on the counter. Her whole body glowed with anticipation. And she was a businesswoman, this could be a good sale on a quiet day.

"Kate, you go home, I'll finish off with this customer and cash up. See you in the morning."

Kate nodded, smiled and disappeared, not needing to be told twice.

"Follow me," Christina adopted his tone of authority. Glancing over her shoulder as she walked to the back of the shop, she could see he was following, as instructed. He appeared to be watching the swing of her hips in her tight pencil skirt.

"Wait there," she said as she closed the changing room door behind her. The space was small, just room for two people, in case a customer had a friend with her, or required a second opinion. There were floor to ceiling mirrors against one wall. The other walls were painted a rich cream.

The spotlight overhead gave the customer the best possible light. Not too harsh, but bright enough to show Christina's beautiful products off to their best advantage. Not used to being the customer, Christina felt unsure for a moment. Then, taking a deep breath she undid the zip on her skirt, slid it to the ground and stepped out of it. Standing in front of the mirrors for a moment she appraised herself from the front and rear. Dressed in black French knickers she stocked in the shop, she felt good. She slowly unbuttoned her blouse. Her breasts were high and firm in a pretty matching plunge bra. She unfastened the bra, and pulled the knickers off. Now she stood naked in front of the mirror. Naked all but for four-inch back patent court shoes. She felt slutty, but good too. Her body was toned but curvy, a woman's body. The kind of woman the underwear she sold was designed for.

"Are you ready?" His voice called from the other side of the door.

"Nearly," she replied. "Wait, please."

She wondered if this was how he really wanted to see her. Naked and hot. Parting her legs slightly she stroked her mound, touching her lips, feeling her juices flow over her fingers. She trembled. Yes, she was ready, almost. Gently, Christina slowly pulled the French knickers up. The silk slid effortlessly over her smooth skin, sending tiny electric shocks down her thighs. The bra cupped her breasts beautifully, creating cleavage. If showing him this didn't sell the set, nothing would, thought Christina. She took a deep breath, turned round and pulled the door open.

"So do you think she'll like it?"

He was silent. Appraising me again, thought Christina. She wondered how she measured up.

"Turn around. I need to see you from the back."

She turned from him and leant forward, resting her hands against the mirror. Her breath was warm, frosting the glass. She gazed into her own eyes. She hoped that, for now, they were unreadable.

"Good," his voice was close; she could feel his breath on her shoulder. Glancing at his reflection, and then back to her own, the contrast was striking. He was wearing a charcoal, light wool suit. It looked darker than it was against her pale, uncovered skin.

"Down more, please." This felt like an order. She could feel the silk taut against her arse. She walked her hands down the mirror. Her breasts fell forwards, almost tumbling from the bra. Her nipples rubbed against the lacy edging. The sensation was delicious. She rocked slightly from side to side to heighten the feeling.

"Good, that helps. May I touch?"

She nodded her assent to him in the mirror. Then she felt his hands rove over her silk-encased arse. An electric tingle shot down the back of her thighs. She held her breath. She was damp now, her juices running at the thought of his hands exploring further. But she didn't dare move. She didn't want to break the spell. Superficially it appeared he had power over her. He was clothed, she was almost naked. But she thought she was in charge, that she was gaining the upper hand. She was almost certain now she could dictate his next move. And whatever that move it would lead to pleasure for her, she would be sure of that. And he would need to acquire any pleasure of his own from pleasing her.

He slid his finger inside the leg of the knickers. She gasped with pleasure. That was exactly what she'd hoped he would do.

"Good to see they fit snugly, but access is not denied," he whispered.

She pushed herself back onto his hand, hoping he would insinuate his finger into her soft folds, allow her juices to run down to his wrist. Just the thought was making her clit tingle, her nipples harden more. Then he pulled his hand away and stood up. He wasn't going was he, not now?

"I'm going to take your bra off. I need to see how the clasp works."

"Fine."

Deftly he unfastened her bra with one hand.

"You've done this before, haven't you?"

He didn't smile. Her bra fell to the floor and her breasts fell forward, her nipples proud. She started to pull her hands away from the mirror, to cup her breasts, but he anticipated this movement.

"Stop."

She kept her hands where they were and he reached round her body and took the weight of both breasts in his hands. Now she knew she was definitely in charge. If she hadn't made that attempt at modesty he wouldn't now be caressing and squeezing her breasts, pinching her nipples, delivering the sweetest pain. She threw her head back, he nuzzled into her neck, she breathed deeply, inhaling his scent, maleness blending with expensive cologne. Just as it should be.

His hands slid away from her breasts, brushing down her smooth skin to her waist, reaching the top of her knickers. His next obstacle.

"They're coming off too," he said; unnecessarily, she thought.

He quickly pulled them down to her ankles and she stepped out of them, steadying herself against the mirror, as she teetered momentarily in her heels. He picked them up and threw them into the corner of the tiny room.

"Bend forward again, please. And open your legs."

She did so. His fingers ran down the curve of her hips and round her arse. He had the lightest touch. He reached between her legs.

"You're wet."

Surely he wasn't surprised? She didn't reply. Deftly his

fingers parted her folds and thrust themselves deep into her cunt. The suddenness of this movement made her gasp with delight.

"Am I hurting you?"

She shook her head. He twisted and turned thrusting as deeply as the opening folds of her cunt would allow. She pushed against him. She could feel herself spasm and close around his fingers. Her head and upper body began to move, almost involuntarily, in a slow, silent, sinuous dance. Pulling one hand away from the mirror, steadying herself with the other, she reached down to her clit, and began rubbing it with two fingers, increasing her pleasure. Her fingers touched his, just for a second, then they moved apart. He continued to thrust inside her, filling her. This felt so fucking good. Throwing back her head, she caught a glimpse of her face in the mirror. Her desire widened her eyes, made her skin gleam, added to the fullness of her lips. She knew she was close now to complete surrender. She rubbed her fingers faster over her clit, gliding first gently, then applying more pressure as the sweetest pleasure of her orgasm threatened to overwhelm her.

"Harder, faster." She was the one to issue instructions now. And he obeyed, matching her rhythm, pulling her right hip against him with his free hand. Her skin rubbed against the cool wool of his suit. The slight friction brought her closer still. Beyond the point at which she could control her own body. Christina groaned as her cunt tightened and released with waves of surrender as her orgasm shuddered through her whole body. She felt as though she was on fire. For these moments at least, she was his. Her legs trembled as wave followed wave until gradually the intensity began to subside. Slowly he withdrew his hands. She felt herself spasm again, one final, sweet feeling. Then he took a step back from her. They looked at each other's reflections in the mirror, she held his gaze. He looked down at the reflection of her body. She wondered if, in his eyes, she looked different now. She certainly felt so. Alive and on fire, every nerve ending tingled. Only now she wondered if he had derived pleasure from their encounter. Wondered too if she would ever see him again. She wanted to see what was hidden behind his cool exterior. Wanted to fuck him too.

"The bra and French knickers are perfect. I'll take them. I'll wait at the counter." He left the changing room. She took her time getting dressed, savouring the pleasure her body had just enjoyed.

She joined him at the counter, fully dressed now, and began to wrap the set, her hands trembling slightly. He gave her notes, she rang up the till and handed him the parcel.

"Thank you. Your gift wrapping service is perfect," he said.

She smiled and nodded.

"Glad to be of service."

"I'll return. Next week, maybe. I have it in mind that she would like stockings and a basque too."

He turned and left the shop. Christina's day had turned out unexpectedly well.

Waiting For A Spanking
by Shanna Germain

I'm bent over the kitchen counter, skirt pulled up over my ass, waiting for Doug to come. I don't mean in a sexual way – at least, not yet. I mean, this is the way he told me to wait for him while he drives home from his office. It gives him a thrill, I guess, imagining me here in my black heels and baby blue thong, hands pressed to the Formica, showing my bare ass to the stove and the spice rack while he's fighting traffic on the highway.

This morning, Doug rolled over and whispered what he wanted in my ear: Blue thong – the satin one. My short black work skirt, hiked up. White button-down top, only one button buttoned, no bra. Heels, he didn't care which. Me, ready and waiting, just as he stepped out of his office, an hour's drive away.

I thought about faking it, you know, just waiting until I heard his car pull into the drive before actually getting into position. But this whole spanking thing was my idea, my dream, so I'm willing to play by whatever rules he sets.

See, I'm a spanking kind of girl. Always have been. I love the feel a hand coming down hard on my ass, of a heated palm print on the back of my thighs. That's what first attracted me to Doug – those big hands of his, wide as pancake flippers. Twice as strong.

"What do you do?" I'd asked the night we met at a

friend's house. I couldn't take my eyes of those long fingers wrapped around the fragile stem of a wine glass, the ring that wasn't a wedding ring, the ropy muscles that jumped in his wrists and forearms.

Doug looked those gold-brown eyes into mine. "It's boring," he said. But a grin twitched at one side of his lips. "I'm a rehab therapist. I spend my days whipping people into shape."

I couldn't resist anymore. I put my hand over his, pressed my palm into those wide knuckles. "Tell me about it," I said. "Please."

And that's how we started dated. But through it all, I couldn't get him to spank me. For two months, I flashed my ass every time we got naked, but he didn't take the hint. At least not like that. Not once. I even dug up my copy of *The Compleat Spanker* and accidentally left it around my apartment for him to find. Nothing.

Not that the sex was bad, mind you. It wasn't. Doug knew how to use his hands, outside me, inside me. But through it all, I ached for those big wide hands against my ass in a way I wasn't sure I could articulate. But finally, I did.

Doug was on his side, half-buried beneath the blankets, facing me. I traced the lines in his big paw of a palm with my fingernail. "Have you ever wanted to use these hands for anything, well, harder?" I asked.

Doug took his hand from me, looked at it as though for the first time. "Harder than what?" he asked.

He looked so innocent about it all that I felt my cheeks get hot. I pulled the covers up over my head, inhaled his after-sex smell of sea salt and musk. "Harder than a foot massage?" My words were muffled.

Doug buried his own head under the covers next to me until we were face to face in the semi-darkness. "Is this like that 'bigger than a breadbox' game?" he asked.

"No," I said. My cheeks were burning, but under the cover of darkness, where I could feel his hands but not see them, I asked him for what I wanted, for what I'd wanted since the first time I saw those fingers wrapped around fragile glass.

Even under the blankets, I could see his eyes go a little whiter around the edges. But then he said, "Let me think about it." And that was it. He didn't say anything else about it. Not another word. Not for three weeks. I was sure I'd pushed him too far, too fast. Sure I'd asked for something that was just too far outside of his sexual arsenal.

And then, this morning. Doug rolling over and whispering instructions in my ear before he left for work. He never said the word, never mentioned my request, but I could feel it there between us as his lips brushed against my ear, telling me what to do.

So now, here I am. Bare-assed and bent over the kitchen counter. Hands flat on the Formica. Every inch of my skin is so alive that it's tingling. Waiting…and waiting. And waiting.

By the time I finally hear the key in the front door, I've been waiting an hour and a half. Long after he should have been home, even in bad traffic. My calves are tired. My feet are cranky too, in these heels. My shirt pulls tight across my shoulders. Even my back is starting to ache. And my head, well, my head's thinking maybe this wasn't such a good idea. Maybe we're overdoing it for his first time.

But before I can get any kind of coherent words out, Doug's sliding a piece of fabric over my eyes, his fingers fumbling at the knot at the back of my head. That's all it takes, is the thought of those fingers, of those palms, on me, anywhere on me and I'm not feeling anything but the tingle and ache of want.

A plastic bag rustles on the ground near my feet. The clunk and clatter of things as Doug sets them on the countertop next to me. The smell of something fresh and wet, like dewy grass, fills my nose. "What–"

"No talking," Doug says. His voice is lower than usual. Harsher, trying to get into a tough guy persona. But it comes out all wrong. You can hear him trying too hard. I lay my cheek down against the cool of the countertop to bury my giggle. To laugh now would ruin everything.

But then he puts his hands on my skin and I forget about laughing. He presses his palms right on the fleshy part of my ass. His skin is cold from the outside and the thin strip of his metal ring is even colder, and I jump a little. Doug starts out pretty good. He uses those hands to caress the curves of my ass, smooth solid strokes from under the waistband of my skirt down to the backs of my thighs. Stroke, stroke, his hands warming up as they work the distance from my lower back to my knees.

He taps my ass with his fingertips. And then again. I'm not even sure he's touching me, it's so light. I focus hard on the feeling in my ass – yes, there it is again, just the tiniest of tap-taps. He's either scared of hurting me or afraid of his own desires, so he just keeps tapping his way around my ass like a blind man with a cane.

Then he goes back to stroking the skin with a gentle touch. Very, very gentle. So gentle I can barely feel it. He must have learned this warm-up technique from the book, but I think he's overdoing it a little. It's warmed up, Doug, I want to yell, holy crap, hit it already. But I promised I'd do this his way. No talking, no giving orders, so he doesn't get nervous.

Instead, I lean my ass as far back as I can, trying to get my skin closer to his hands. C'mon, c'mon, I think, give me a good wap for Christ's sakes. But I don't want to freak him out either. Damn, I'm barely wet and now my back is starting to ache again from bending over.

He's not touching me anymore. Silence and then a

strange crunch from behind me. Something being snapped in two. Something wet trails beneath the curve of my cheek. Like brushing through damp leaves. It drags across my skin, wet and limp. What the hell is that, a piece of limp celery? I concentrate all my senses on that part of my ass, feel the drag and pull of the wet against it. When he drags it between my legs, cold and a little harder, I realise that, yes, it is celery. And not only is it limp, it's cold and wet too. I don't remember *that* from the book.

A little sting against the side of my right cheek. I feel it before I hear it, the thwap of the celery. Not so light and limp this time. A stripe of almost-pain blooms there and then fades, fast. I wait for more. Instead, I hear the snap again. And then Doug's hands around the front of me, pulling my shirt open, dragging wet and cold leaves across my nipples until they pucker and ache against the cold. He presses my back down until my whole front is against the counter, against the celery stalks. One for each nipple. My nipples slide into the wet grooves of the celery.

"Stay there," Doug says. This time his voice is his own, gravelly only from desire. He brings one hand between my legs, pressing there through my panties, finding the moisture and grinding his finger against it just long enough for me to really, really want him to do it more. And then he stops.

Across the fleshy part of my ass, a little bloom of pain. Soft. Only this time it's not fingers, but cloth. The sound is loud, thwap, louder than the feeling. He hits me again, light, on the back of my thigh. Just a soft touch of fabric. A whisper. Not even. They're apron strings. He got that from the book too. But he hasn't tied knots or beads in the end – he must not have read that far.

He reaches around and tucks one of the apron strings between my legs. He pulls up until it barely touches my clit. I press down against it, and the fabric gives, bending with me, never allowing me to really feel it pressing there. Not as hard as I want it to. Not hard enough.

A surge of anger rises in my stomach, in my hands that become fists against the counter. I want to yank the stupid blindfold off and show him how to use those hands, please, please…Jesus Christ, I think, how hard is it to spank a person?

And that's when he brings the round end of the wooden spoon down hard against my ass. "Fuck!" It's the first thing I've said in hours and it feels good coming out my mouth. He could have fucking warned me.

I'm about ready to turn around and call it quits when I realise my cunt is throbbing. That in truth, it has been since we started. Thirty minutes of me standing here thinking he's not doing it right, and the whole time I'm so turned on I'm practically dripping on the floor.

A second later, he's got the handle of that wooden spoon against my clit and he's finally, finally hammering one of those big flat hands against my ass. Right over the spot that's still aching from the wooden spoon. One of those big hands nails me again and again, right on that sweet, tender spot, and the other hold the handle of that wooden spoon hard against my clit. My ass is on fire. My clit too. I know he told to be quiet, but I have to cry out. Everything feels. So. Fucking. Good.

I can't tell where he's hitting me and where he's not anymore. Every part of me tingles and burns. The fire that started in my ass and cunt rises through me, hot and crackling, searing my skin, my mind. Consuming me.

After a minute, I can breathe again. My ass feels like I backed into the oven, but the rest of me is tired, sated, empty.

Doug pulls the blindfold off my eyes and turns me around to face him, brushing my skirt gently down over my burning ass. "Is that kind of what you were hoping for?" he asks. There's a little grin twitching at one side of his mouth, the same way it was on the night we met.

I suddenly get it. The over-the-top innocence. The soft strokes. The, I'll-give-it-a-try spiel. "You are a total sandbagger," I say. "I can't believe you did that."

Doug doesn't disagree. Just reaches those wide hands around to softly cup my ass. "Let's just say I've had plans for this ass since the first time I saw it."

Sparring Partners
by Everica May

"Ai!"

I landed the kick on the side of Riz's helmet, slid back and round-kicked him in the chestguard.

"Ai!"

His spinning hook kick barely missed my face and I followed with a round kick directly into his exposed *hogu*.

"Ai!"

I could tell he was getting frustrated, but there was no one to pause the match. Master Kim had given me the key to the *dojang* so that Riz and I could practise, with the understanding that there would be no one to referee us. The tournament was in two weeks, and we both wanted to hone our skills some more in preparation.

A shock went through my head as Riz got in a beautiful inside kick on my helmet. How frustrating! I lit him up with a succession of three rapid round kicks, followed by a jumping spinning back kick that knocked him down. I guess I was a little angry.

When Riz got up, the thought passed through my mind that maybe we should stop before things got out of control. I had always found Riz pretty hot, and was enjoying the sparring session alone with him, but we were both so competitive that I could see this getting a little crazy if we weren't careful. I took out my mouthguard.

"Wait," I said. "I'm sorry. That was uncalled for."

He shook his head, grinning. "It was a perfectly legitimate hit."

He waited for me to replace my mouthguard, then closed the distance between us with a cross-step side kick that sent me banging into the wall. He followed closely so that I couldn't regain a good kicking posture and pinned me against the wall, pressing his chestguard against mine. A mischievous spark came into his eyes.

"Give up?" he asked

"Mat Hang!" I said, grinning – *Your mama*! – the only Malay he'd taught me that I could ever seem to remember. I punched his chestguard, pushing him away, and launched a flurry of ferocious kicks that sent him reeling backwards across the *dojang* floor. That may have been a mistake, because then I was dying for air. Riz countered, a fierce light in his eye, and I moved to block, but tripped and fell backwards. In an instant he was on top of me.

I looked up into his face and saw the expression in his black eyes change from frustrated determination to something quite different. He ripped out his mouthguard and stared into my eyes. I was frozen there, pinned, yes, by his weight, but also transfixed by that look. Slowly, I took out my own mouthguard, staring into his eyes all the while. He removed his helmet, revealing his short, black hair slicked down with sweat, then reached down and undid the strap on my own helmet and pulled it off. Neither of us spoke, both of us staring at each other in a kind of surprised wonder. I sometimes fantasized about Riz, but having the fantasies come true was a bit shocking, really. Maybe he was experiencing the same sort of thing.

Slowly, still looking into my eyes, he bent down and put his mouth on mine.

I had already been short of breath and pumped up on adrenaline. Now I could feel my heart hammering in my throat and could hardly breathe. I started to bring my hands up to push Riz off, but he grabbed both my wrists, forced them to the floor beside my head, and continued kissing me.

A small whimper escaped me. I knew this was wrong, but I wanted it so much. What if we got caught? What if someone passing by on the sidewalk looked in? Abruptly, Riz rolled off of me and stood. I laid there for a moment, panting, then got to my feet and faced him.

We stared at each other, motionless, for a moment. Then Riz looked up toward the glass door and back at me. He walked over to the bank of light switches on the wall and with a pass of his hand flicked them all off. Now the only light came from the two emergency exit signs and the various shop lights outside.

Riz walked slowly, deliberately toward me. I backed up a couple of steps, watching his eyes, wanting him but hesitant, and found myself against the wall. He kept coming, pressed his chestguard against mine and leaned in to kiss me again. My skin was prickling with excitement and I knew my face was flushed – it felt like it was glowing. I couldn't get away even if I wanted to. And I didn't want to.

Suddenly Riz grabbed my chestguard and pulled me away from the wall, spinning me around. I felt him tugging at the ties behind me and then my *hogu* dropped to the floor. I turned to see him undoing his own straps and shedding his chestguard as well. He moved forward, backing me into the wall again, and now I could feel the hardness of his muscular chest as he pressed against me, his black eyes half taunting, half desirous.

With a moan, I gave in and bent forward, kissing his neck, tasting the saltiness of his skin. I grabbed him and pulled him closer, becoming more desperate for him with each moment. I tried to grind my sex against him, but we were both wearing protective cups. Grabbing the waistband of my own cup, I shoved it down, then pulled his down as well, smashing myself against him, rolling my hips, panting with desire. He was so hard, he may as well have still been wearing the cup.

Backing away a step, he reached down for my hand, slowly pulling off my armpad while watching my face. My throat was too tight for me to speak, so I merely stared back into his eyes hoping that he would understand how much I wanted this. After slipping off my other armpad, he pulled off his own with swift, sure movements.

I stood, frozen, overwhelmed by the desire to step in and kiss him, to touch his face, to tear off his shirt, but uncertain where to start. Riz made the decision for me by ripping off his own shirt and then peeling mine slowly off over my head. He pulled my sports bra off next and we stood there, naked from the waist up, sweaty, breathing hard. My eyes had adjusted to the semi-darkness and I could see the fine sheen of sweat on his well-defined chest and abdomen, red and blue glints reflected in it from the lights outside. The air felt very cool on my skin. My nipples were standing out hard and erect and I could feel the sweat trapped under the lower curves of my breasts.

Riz stepped forward again, placing his hot hands on my waist, mouth finding mine again. He slid his hands around behind me, then pushed them down under my waistband, under my panties and grabbed both cheeks firmly, pulling me closer, pressing his hardness against me.

Unable to wait any longer, I grabbed his waistband, making sure to get his underwear as well, and hauled downward, freeing his throbbing erection. I grasped it, feeling his heat in my hand, thrilling as it pulsated against my fingers. I felt the blood engorging my clitoris and I gasped as I imagined what he would feel like inside of me. I pulled away from him and dropped to my knees, taking him into my mouth, savouring the hot saltiness of him, his musky, masculine smell. I took him deep into my throat and he moaned and grabbed the back of my head.

Someone yanked on the locked door, rattling it loudly. We both froze, then dropped to the floor behind the half-wall that separated the viewing area from the training floor. I crawled to the end of the half wall and peeked around to look at the door just in time to see a figure reeling unsteadily away.

"It's OK," I breathed. "Just some drunk."

I let out a sigh of relief, then gasped loudly as Riz pierced me from behind. Grabbing my hips, he thrust rapidly and deeply into me, grunting with the effort of it. Then, as suddenly as he had started he stopped, leaving me aching for more.

I slid back along his cock, drawing in a sharp breath as he reached around and began stroking my clitoris. He let me set the rhythm, sliding back and forth on him as he continued fondling my clit, which was swelling even larger. I could feel the wave of impending orgasm rising, swelling, threatening to wash over me. I pushed back against him hard, gasping at the almost painfully delicious depth of his penetration. And then the wave reared up and crashed down over me and I cried out loudly, jerking back against his hot thighs, feeling his cock bottoming out inside of me.

Shuddering, I slowed my pace and then stopped, panting, exhausted, glowing all over. Riz withdrew and I turned to face him, sitting on the mats. He pushed me back so that I was lying down and moved over me on all fours, looking down at me. He bent down with agonising slowness until his face was only an inch or so from mine. My heart was hammering hard and my breath coming in short gasps in anticipation of what was to come. One of his knees was in between mine, and as he placed his lips on my own, he used his knee to shove my own apart, then positioned his cock at the entrance of my slippery slit. Ever so slowly, he pressed his cock forward into me. Little by little, with maddening slowness, he pushed further in. I was moaning now, crying out, "Oh Riz! Please! Please Riz! I need it all! Please!"

He looked into my eyes.

"Tell me to get off," he said.

"No!" I said. "Please, no. I want more!"

"Tell me to get off," he repeated.

I could see so deeply into his eyes that I felt I had touched his soul, and at that moment I understood what he wanted. I writhed beneath him, pulling away from his cock even though every part of me was screaming out to impale myself further on him.

"Get off!" I cried. I slapped at him, and he caught my hand, forcing it down to the mats.

I put more effort into my squirming, trying to roll out from under him and feeling with delicious terror that I was truly trapped.

"Get off," I cried out again. "Let me go!"

I slapped at him with my other hand and he pinned that one to the mats as well.

Now I was twisting underneath him but he was so strong that I could move barely a millimetre. His hands around my wrists felt like iron vices clamping me to the floor. His thighs were pinning my own to the ground and I was helpless.

"Get off!" I screamed, but I knew from the hungry look in his eye that he could see the desire in my own. And then his cock stabbed into me, sudden and sharp and white-hot. I cried out in ecstasy and he began fucking me in earnest. His breath was coming in short gasps, his sweat trickling down over me and mingling with my own. I was out of control beneath him, now, crying out, writhing, screaming. I could feel that he was close to coming and all I wanted was for him to come deep inside of me.

His movements became more urgent and then with a

loud shout he was slamming into me, erupting inside of me, filling me with his seed.

Utterly spent, he rolled over, bringing me on top of him. I stretched out along his naked body, pressing against his wet, spent cock and laying my head in the hollow of his neck and shoulder. We breathed together in silence, basking in the afterglow, thrilled and a little shocked by what we'd done.

Finally, he sighed.

"I think we need more practice," he said, his fingers trailing gently across the side of my breast.

I grinned, nuzzling his neck.

"We definitely need more practice."

Possession
by Penelope Friday

She was aware of him from the moment she entered the room. She took one quick look around to gauge his position; then, once it was fixed in her mind, she turned to her nearest companion and started a desultory conversation. She had dressed not so much to attract as to pique his interest. Her usually unruly red hair was severely clipped up; her figure confined by a dress that hinted at more than it exposed. He would see and he would... wonder.

She knew when he spotted her. She was laughing with another man when she felt (felt, rather than saw) him looking at her. She cast a glance to her left, caught his eye only in passing, and returned to her conversation. She knew he was not deceived.

But it was later – much later – before their paths crossed. The chatting, giggling party continued around her, but suddenly there was a grasp on her wrist; a long-fingered, masculine hand that pulled her quickly away and into a side room. She noticed the sumptuous velvet cushions on the couch; the heavy, expensive curtains at the window, and smiled at the ostentatious trappings of wealth. That was one way he would not impress her.

"Hello, Rafael," she said coolly, ignoring the suddenly quickened beating of her heart.

He was tall. He was blond. He was used to women (and,

most probably, men) falling at his feet at one glance. He would have to work for Ana's adoration. She hoped he was intending to do so.

"You came, then."

"Oh yes, I came." She shrugged elegant black clad shoulders. "I was interested to see how the other half live."

He still kept that grasp on her wrist; and he moved closer so that they were side by side.

"No. Oh no, Ana. You came to see me."

"You think so?" Her tone was light. She would not let him see how much his closeness affected her.

"Mm-hm. I told you that I would have you; that you would lie down for me, and you would let me do as I wanted with your body. And here you are. How convenient."

She lifted her chin, and took a step towards the door as if to leave, but his grasp of her wrist prevented her going further. Instead, she found herself tugged back into his arms, her right arm pinioned behind her against the wall.

"Oh," she said huskily, "so you're going to make me."

The sounds of the party drifted through the closed door. A crash: someone had dropped a champagne flute, she thought irrelevantly.

"No. I'm going to make you beg."

His words made her catch her breath as she looked the few inches up into his face. Their bodies were so close that her breasts pressed up against his shirt front. Her lips were tingling with her desperation for him to kiss her, but she would not make the first move. There was a deep voiced remark from the other side of the door, and a burst of laughter that shot through her. It was as if all her senses were in a state of hyper-awareness.

"Really?" She fought to keep her voice steady, cynical.

He looked at her for a second and she felt her body flush with heat. She thought that she might be trembling, then realised that it was the impatient beating of her heart. With deliberate slowness, he lowered his lips to hers in a quick, teasing kiss. Her right hand he still held behind her, but her left crept up to his head, to pull him into a deeper embrace. Smiling, he resisted her advances, keeping a small teasing distance between them.

"You look very prim with your hair up like that," Rafael murmured. "Prim and proper. But we both know that is not the real Ana Fitzpatrick, don't we?"

His hand threaded into her hair, tugging auburn tendrils free of their bindings until they curled around her cheekbones and down onto her shoulders.

"There," he said, with warm satisfaction. "Now you look more like the wanton Ana I know."

The hand moved a little lower, sliding the sleeves of the black dress down so that two pale white shoulders were exposed. This time she did shiver, as his fingertips brushed lightly over her shoulder blades.

"What… if I say no?"

One eyebrow lifted, and the smile quirked onto his face again.

"Are you going to?"

There was another rumble of voices. The party was continuing only inches from where they stood. Those people had no idea…

"What if someone comes in?"

"By the time I've finished with you, you won't care if they're all watching," he promised her. He saw she still hesitated, and added, "But I see you still need a little persuasion…"

He kissed her again, releasing her arm from behind her as he did so. He was, Ana realised, deliberately giving her the opportunity to break away: he knew as well as she that she would not. His lips were firm against hers; his tongue delicate and suggestive as he explored her mouth. His hands were on her shoulders; she imagined them leaving burn marks where they touched, such was the heated effect on her. The hands slipped lower down her arms, taking the sleeves of her dress with them until the upper curves of her breasts lay exposed to him. One muscular leg slipped between hers, pushing the satin skirt of the dress up between her thighs to rub against her. He shifted; shifted again and the pressure lowered then increased until she found it hard to concentrate, to think, to *breathe*.

His mouth moved across her cheek towards her ear, leaving a trail of white hot kisses where it touched.

"Shall I stop, Ana?"

"Yes," she breathed, meaning *No* – desperately meaning no – but as yet too proud to say it.

He kissed her neck, one hand gently teasing the loose strands of her hair out of his way to allow him access to every pleasure. His thigh was hard between her legs and she sighed softly and leant further in towards him. His left hand stroked her back, slowly and rhythmically.

"You are sure you want me to stop?" he pressed.

His hands were both lowered now, cupping the curves of her bottom; pulling her against him so that she could feel how hard, how erect, he was.

"Yes…" keened Ana.

"'Yes', what?"

Rafael rocked her on his leg until she gasped and gasped again.

"Stop – oh, stop." Ana's hands were locked behind his neck, holding him close. Her mouth sought his for another kiss, her arousal clear.

"Very well." Rafe's voice was amused.

He lifted his hands to hers, unclasping that desperate grasp from him. Then, as he stepped away, he ran fingertips over the front of her body, making obvious the hard tips of her nipples, and setting up a tingle that had an echo lower down her body. Then he stepped back, and Ana could feel him looking at her.

She knew what he must see: cheeks flushed pink with desire, hair escaping over her shoulders in a riot of ginger curls (her hairclip had long been discarded on the floor), body yearning – positively reaching out – for his touch. But she would not; she *would not* beg.

"Rafe..."

"You only have to say," he said softly.

She felt almost dizzy, made light-headed by his withdrawal.

"I... don't..." She could not continue.

"I think you do."

Rafael reached out a hand to her hot cheek, smoothing his fingers across her face. Ana was almost frightened by the fierce desire to rip his suit from him, to run her tongue and fingers over every contour of his body – to make him lust for her with the same intensity that she desired him. There was a sudden bang against the door, and she jumped; her hands reaching up to cover her breasts, although she had seen women at the party with dresses that exposed more than she did even now. Rafe laughed.

"You are so nervous, my dear. Someone slipped – that is all."

"Slipped..." She mouthed the word as if she did not understand its meaning.

"Yes, slipped," mocked Rafe. "As I could... slip... your dress from you: over your shoulders, down across your breasts to your hips. And then further..."

He was matching his actions to his words: her black dress was already around her waist and she had made no move, no sound, to tell him 'no'. Had not even considered doing so – she was desperate for his touch.

"Yes..." The word was out of her mouth before she realised she'd spoken. Barely conscious of the flimsy black bodice that was all that now protected her modesty, she was reaching out to him, her fingers stiff and awkward as she fought, half-blind, with the buttons on his shirt.

"Yes?"

"Yes – Rafael!" Almost, she was past the moment of turning back. Almost.

His hands reached up behind her, feeling for the clasps of that already revealing corset. His lips brushed against hers with teasing gentleness.

"You want me?" he asked.

"You know I do."

Pretence was gone now: left in its place was a desperate, hungry urgency. She pushed his jacket and his shirt away, pressing her mouth to his chest, breathing in the scent of his masculinity, running her tongue over the solid arc of his rib cage.

"Please..." she whispered, and felt her bodice fall from her, leaving her nude; nude and *wanting*.

She was still aware of the dull clamour of the crowd, so close to where they stood; yet they had ceased to matter. Rafael had said that it would be so, and he was right. He was all that mattered; that and the way he made her feel. His fingers were on her breasts, teasing the pointed nubs until the stood out ever firmer, and her hands clutched convulsively at his shoulders. He had pushed her hair to one side and his mouth was warm and sensuous on her neck, making her arch her back in mute pleasure.

"Do you like that?"

"Oh yes – yes!"

She was unbuttoning his trousers, pushing them down impatiently and pulling him against her.

"Ana?" She looked up, and he was gazing down at her, mouth serious, eyes dancing. "What if someone comes in?"

Her words, thrown back at her. She gave a desperate glance at the door and then pulled him close again.

"Please?"

"'Please' what, Ana? Should I stop?"

"No... Oh God, Rafe..." She knew what he wanted; couldn't bear to withhold it any longer. "Please, I'm begging you..."

"Anything you want, he said, his hands stroking her back and down her bottom. "You just have to ask. That is all."

'All,' he said. But he knew, and she knew too, what would lie beneath such a request. He was asking her to give – eagerly and unstintingly – all power, all control into his hands: demanding submission, total, willing submission, in return for... in return for what? His mouth was heated on hers; the blood tingled in her lips; throbbed between her thighs. In return for *this* – pure, undiluted ecstasy; a tiny glimpse of heaven. And she could not – did not *want* to – resist, especially when she saw the tender look in his eyes that promised that her submission would harness his: that by handing power to him, she became the more powerful. He would be in thrall to her as much as she to him.

"Well, my Ana?"

"Touch me. Touch me, please. Make love to me."

Her eyes were on his, her face flushed with anticipation, her expression open and trusting. She would give her body over to him, for him to treat as he would. She would kneel for him, beg for him, submit to him. She would love every second of it.

"And the others?"

The champagne was clearly flowing in the next room: voices were getting louder; occasional bursts of music could be heard.

"I don't give a damn about them," she said deliberately.

She knelt down before him, removing his shoes and socks before peeling down his trousers. She pressed her mouth to each foot in turn before moving the kisses higher; up his calves, tongue licking at the backs of his knees; small nibbling bites on the insides of his thighs. One single kiss to the very tip of his erection.

"I want you. Please, Rafe."

Her lips were slightly parted, her hands reaching up to hold his hips.

"I knew you were not so prim," he teased lovingly. "How could I refuse a lady who asks so nicely?"

He stripped his jacket and shirt off and stood naked in front of her.

"Oh."

It was barely a word, more an exhaled breath as her throat seemed suddenly constricted. She had known that he was beautiful. She had known it – but now, kneeling there, a wave of longing washed over her more strongly still.

"Last chance to turn back," Rafael said quietly; but mutely she shook her head.

No, she did not want to change her mind. She wanted his body hard against hers; wanted to explore every different texture of his skin; to feel him move inside her until she could not help but spasm around him.

"Please – *please!*" she implored desperately, her hands pulling him down towards her, unable to wait longer for what she had desired for so long.

And he laughed softly, and knelt beside her, skin against skin from shoulder to hip, one of his hands in the hair at the back of her neck, the other gathering her in, pulling her closer, kissing her so hard that she felt a trickle of blood on her tongue; a metallic taste of passion. He slipped a hand between her legs, fingers stroking – almost tickling – the slick, wet area so that she bent her face down, biting into his shoulder in a desperate attempt to keep her pleasure silent. They were so close that she could feel his body quivering with laughter; and she dug her fingernails deep into his back.

"Yes?" he asked.

"More – harder – firmer..." And Ana scratched her nails down his back, her hair tumbling into her eyes, over her shoulders, onto his. "Please."

The last word was louder than any of their previous conversation, and she was shocked into a sudden remembrance of their situation; the proximity of so many strangers. They both paused for a second, the fear of discovery once more in mind; but it seemed that no party-goers had any interest in anything outside their room.

"Please," she whispered again, loosening her grip and pushing her curls from her face.

He slid a finger inside her, then another, rocking his wrist so that the pressure came and went and she could do nothing except moan her desire against his chest.

"Like that?"

"Mmm... mmm – but I want you, Rafe – you inside me. Please."

He pushed her gently so that she was lying on the floor, and he was over her.

"What do you want, Ana?"

"You – you... Oh God, Rafe, fuck me. I need you; I need – ah..."

He had thrust into her wet depths and the tremor rocked through her. Her breasts rose and fell with her gasping breaths.

"You're *mine*, Ana."

He was claiming her with words as well as with his body; making certain of her submission. She nodded: the moment for words for her had passed; all her concentration was on the feeling; the relinquishing of control, of restraint, for the attainment of a far greater prize. She rocked her hips back and forth, but he held her down, her wrists pinned to the floor either side of her head.

"Mine," he reminded her.

"Yes." It was just a breath of a word.

And he was moving – moving – and her eyes flickered shut as her senses overloaded. Determined to keep quiet, she yet could not prevent the tiny noises of arousal that caught in her throat. It was summer lightning; it was stormy seas; it was a climax that ran through her leaving her spent, her eyes opening in time to see his moment of ecstatic orgasm flash across his face.

His expensive possessions had left her cold; the pure heat of his possession was beyond price.

The Gift
by Dolores Day

Lady Marskbury was unhappy. She seldom smiled, of course she was always polite and
no one could ever accuse her of ever being rude or unpleasant. There was just something in her demeanour that indicated a generally melancholy.

Some young bucks laughed about it. Who could blame the lady for being miserable seeing as how she was married to Fredrick, Lord Marskbury? The lord was an inveterate gambler, quite addicted to cards and he was all of thirty years his wife's senior. Many a young buck would have liked to try his hand at wooing the lady but she repulsed all advances with disdain.

The Countess Lambertz, on a two months visit from Saxony, had the answer to Lady Marskbury's problem. It was she who guessed what the matter with Susanna was. Taking the young girl under her wing, the Countess befriended Susanna and offered her friendship, which was just what the lonely girl craved.

"You are a long way from home, Susanna and I am sure you must miss New York society. It is so stuffy here, don't you think?"

Susanna sighed. "Not really stuffy. I mean New York society can be stuffy too, it's just…" she shrugged her slender shoulders.

But the Contessa was wise enough not to push the girl further, instead she concentrated on building her trust. Once that was gained the Contessa was certain that Susanna would tell her what the matter really was.

Susanna's revelation came almost too late. Contessa Lambertz was returning to Saxony within twenty four hours. Perhaps it was her friend's imminent departure that caused Susanna to burst into tears.

"I shall miss you so much, you have made me so happy," she sobbed, wiping away tears with trembling fingers. "I am so sorry, Leonie, I did not want to do this."

"Nonsense, you should do it more often. I know you have been so unhappy and you are so stoical about it, Susanna, but really you should let it out. It does no good to bottle things up, which is the English way!"

"I can confess I do find them rather *sang froid* and none more so than my husband. Of course he does not love me. I think I always knew that."

"But do you love him?" Leonie asked kindly.

Susanna looked up her blue eyes looked even paler filled as they were with tears. "Oh no! I did not want to marry him but my parents sold me into this marriage. He wanted money and they wanted a title. I didn't want or need either. They have this dream of their grandchildren being of English nobility and through them the name of Harrington will go down in history. That was all *they* cared about. They would not consider my feelings in the matter. They always were hard hearted where I was concerned, preferring my brother but to do this to me…it is unbelievably cruel."

"I must confess he seems an unlikely man for you and now I can see why the marriage was made and why you are so unhappy."

"Oh, he is so dreadful!" Susanna looked around as if to ensure they were alone. Drawing her chair close to Leonie she said, in so a low a voice that Leonie had to strain to hear. "I am still untouched. He does not believe in it. Does not want children and says if I become pregnant he shall cast me out. The whole of society will despise me. He says he will never consummate our marriage and if I tell my parents he will ..." she shook her head as if she could not believe what she was saying. "Have my virginity taken by force."

"What a monstrous thing to threaten."

"Indeed, he is a cruel monster. I do not want to have a child with him – one day I am sure he will die. He drinks so much port and brandy he cannot make old bones! Then I can marry who I like ...oh, Leonie you don't despise me for these wicked thoughts?"

"Of course I don't, my dear. They are perfectly natural. But can you not be a little happy? We have had such good times, going to the theatre and buying pretty things. I take it from this that he is not parsimonious in other ways?"

"Oh no," the young girl sighed. "He likes me to dress well and to have lovely things, it reflects on him. So long as I remain chaste and do not pester him, then I may do as I like but Leonie...*I have feelings*!"

"What kind of feelings, my dear?"

"Oh," the girl sighed and then blushed. "Aches ...tingles..."

"*Throbbing*?"

The girl shot her friend a surprised look. Susanna had wanted to avoid that word but it described precisely the feelings she frequently experienced.

"Sometimes I have the most wonderful dreams..."

"Of course you do and in these dreams the throbbing is increased and sometimes, satisfied?"

"Never the latter. I must not talk this way, please forgive me."

"There is nothing to forgive, my dear. We all have these feelings – obviously not Lord Marskbury – but everyone else. You are young and vital. It is the most natural thing in the word and I think I can help you, if you will permit me?"

Susanna lay in bed, the curtains pulled around the bed, the only light the flicker of the flames dancing on the ceiling. Tonight, warm with the knowledge that her friend had given her, the feelings were more intense than they had ever been. She moved restlessly in the huge bed, uncertain, afraid even.

The agony grew, the throbbing between her tightly-clenched legs, practically unbearable. Slowly, her hand trembling, she pushed up her night gown, pulling it high on her stomach. Tentatively she allowed her hand to move down her belly. The soft brush of hair tickled her palm. Urgently she moved her hand away, back up her stomach. She slid the hand across her stomach, feeling the pulsating rhythm even there in the pit of her belly. Squeezing her eyelids she tried to block out the light – but not only that, she also wished to block out the deed. It was ridiculous; after all she could not see what her wandering hand was doing.

She slid the hand down once more into the curling hair, along the cleft. She felt fleshy lips against her palm. Slowly, feeling her cheeks flood with blood, she parted her legs wide, and as Leonie had said, moved her middle finger over the sensitised folds. A warm gushing sensation pervaded her being, she moaned from the intensity of it. Now she explored each fleshy fold, seeking for the tiny bud, that Leonie promised would bring her such raw pleasure she would end up gasping for air.

Strange, the pouting lips her finger gently stroked awoke a roaring inside her, now she worked two fingers again them, feeling something warm trickle over her fingers. Her hips thrashed on the bed, her breath came in short gasps. One of her fingers found the bud, it was hard and swollen and as she teased it, a frightening pleasure engulfed her, her body pitched and rocked and shuddered as she was transported with delight into a delicious world of intense peaks of pleasure.

And then it was over and she lay spent and tired and blissfully aware that she had found what she had needed.

Susanna was not sure about Arleta. The girl was far too pretty. As a personal maid she seemed perfect but she was not quite certain why the Countess Lambertz had selected her of all girls.

Susanna watched her a good deal of the time, wanting to find fault but unable to do so. Was it the girl's air of confidence that awoke her suspicion? She moved with an ease and elegance that was unusual in a servant. However, the girl was French and perhaps that accounted for it.

"She will be perfect for you," the Countess had insisted. "Trust me in this."

It was because she did trust the Countess that she did not seek another place for Arleta. After all it was because of the Countess that Susanna had discovered such pleasure in the darkness of night. It was she who was unsophisticated, who did not understand the way of European servants, which was why she was always watching Arleta.

In the early morning, drowsy from a blissful sleep, Susanna awakened. She saw the thin sliver of light sneaking in through the bed hanging. His lordship had gone to London and would be gone for months. She did not care. Of course it was quiet here in Somerset but she could ride and even go to Bath if she needed stimulus, but she doubted she would bother. Here she had her books, her piano her horses and of course…she turned on the pillow, lifting her hand she kissed her first and second finger. The warmth started to spread across her stomach in anticipation of her morning ritual. Now with modesty gone, she took off her nightgown and lay nude, kicking aside the silken sheets and parting her legs wide. Teasing herself, she spent time licking her fingers until they were sticky with her saliva, then slowly she lowered her hand, rubbing her damp fingers over her pouting vulva. She smiled in delight and then – light flooded the bed, too startled to move she turned horrified eyes onto…Arleta.

Horrified she cupped her nakedness. "What are you?" she spluttered. "Close the curtains…get out!"

"But my lady, it is too lonely, is it not?" The girl smiled. Her lips were plump and red, a short little tongue shot out moistening them. Fascinated, aware that she was blushing, confused and unsure what to do, feeling herself losing control, Susanna just stared. Her pleasure was gone; she would never dare do this wonderful thing again. She had been caught in her sin.

"My lady, the Countess, she wishes me to look after you, as I have looked after her."

Now the girl stepped closer to the bed, drawing the bed curtains to a close.

"What are you doing? How dare you!"

"My lady, do not be afraid. Please allow me."

"Allow you to…" But the girl moved swiftly, bending her head and putting her plump lips against Susanna's. The kiss was sweet and pleasant and in a moment Susanna relaxed. Kissing was something she enjoyed; she had shared in many a sweet kiss at boarding school with one or other of her girlfriends. But that was all it had been…Arleta's hand was now moving slowly over Susanna's breast, teasing the pink nipple with her thumb. Half aroused, the throbbing petals between her legs, pouted and poured out their sweetness; she felt it trickle between her legs. Part of her wanted to order Arleta to stop but the kisses were so delightful, and that little pointed ruby coloured tongue she had seen, was now teasing her own.

Arleta's hand strayed from Susanna's breast, wandering with circling movements over her stomach, causing Susanna's hips to move against the silken sheets. The fingers sliding over her swollen clitoris caused a far more intense explosion of feeling than her own hand had ever given her. Her mind no longer put up resistance. She gave her body over to Arleta willingly, eagerly.

Susanna spread her legs, lost in the delightfully sensations Arleta's hand was arousing. Now the girl slid her mouth away from her mistresses, her tongue licking down Susanna's body, pausing only to run her tongue around the pouting nipple before sliding down, across her stomach, over the curling, soft, blonde hair.

Susanna moaned and thrashed and then felt the hot little tongue that moments ago had been in her mouth, slide over her moist vulva. The girl took her in her mouth. Susanna screamed in ecstasy. "Suck me, suck me..." she was sobbing, her hips gyrating, the pain was pleasure and the pleasure was pain. Almost she was there...reaching for paradise...

But the girl stopped. Susanna's eyes widened. Arleta came to her. "Unbutton me," she commanded. Susanna obeyed, her fingers trembling so much she could barely open the seemingly hundreds of hooks and eyes. When the dress fell away from her, she saw that Arleta was naked. No petticoats or bloomers, no bodice. She stared at the French girl's body, so slim yet with perfect pointed little breasts, the nipples large and brown. Her belly was flat and below was a silky patch of jet black hair that made the crimson folds of her womanhood vivid.

With a cry, Susanna leapt up, wanting the feel those large nipples in her mouth; she fastened on one, suckling it while her hand clasped the girl's round silky behind.

Arleta rolled her back onto the bed, kneeling over her and still Susanna sucked on the delicious nipple.

Covering Susanna's body with her own, Arleta rubbed her vulva against her mistress'.

"My lady," she murmured, "You are gorgeous and I want to do it to you so much, do you want me to...mm? Do you want to do it to me?"

Sliding her mouth reluctantly from the other girl's nipple, she murmured. "I do...you can do anything to me."

"I can fuck you if you like but the Contessa says you are still a virgin, maybe you will fuck me one day..."

"We cannot..."

The girl chuckled. "Oh yes, my lady we can do anything. I have a delightful play thing. Now my lady, may I call you darling for now...?"

"Oh yes, my love..."

"Then my darling, I will suck you, and you will suck me...come, now," the girl reached up and kissed her lips, her hands sliding in to the damp folds of Susanna. Releasing Susanna's lips, Arleta turned herself around, spreading her legs over her mistress' body, then bending herself to take the warm, yielding petals into her mouth. Susanna writhed, in delight; she could see the delightful moons of her maid's buttocks, and beyond the essence of her. She, with a movement she was hardly aware of, slid her tongue along the crimson centre. As she did she felt Arleta's mouth tighten over her, her tongue with rapid strokes, sliding inside her. Now the girl lowered herself over Susanna, and Susanna, her pleasure mounting pushed her tongue into the girl's opening, in and out with rapid strokes, they were moving together in perfect unison now, Susanna's swiftly reaching that paradise she sought, only this was more intense than she had ever dreamed of...

Everyone remarked on the change in Lady Marskbury. She moved with far more confidence. She was able to hold a conversation with anyone and was known as a gracious hostess.

When Lord Marskbury died from a fall from his horse many expected that after a decent period of mourning that the lady would marry.

Even, when she came on yet another visit, the Countess suggested that her friend might marry again.

"No, I have no intention of marrying. I have all I desire."

The Countess looked at her friend. "Arleta proved to be a good servant, then?"

"Oh yes," Susanna smiled.

"It is not that you have perhaps..."and she whispered, "fallen in love?"

"My dear, Countess, of course I haven't. Arleta is good fun but I am not in love with her."

"I see, but then why would you not marry?"

"And give my parents the satisfaction of grandchildren." Susanna laughed a bitter little laugh. "They gave me in marriage to a man I despised. He wanted only my money, now I have my money and my title. My line shall die with me. There will be no history books that tell of the daring deeds of the offspring of the Marksburys, nor any other lord and Susanna Harrington. Of course they may be a footnote in history. The Marskbury line died because the American woman the last lord married gave him no heirs. But what do I care?" Susanna shrugged. "I have everything I desire, well almost." Susanna smiled.

"And my dear because I have learned something – Arleta taught me well you know, and from time to time – and like tonight for instance...I shall do something that I am fond of. It is something that gives me a great sense of power as well as pleasure."

"You intrigue me."

"She taught me how to fuck, darling and tonight I intend to fuck you!"

"Susanna," the Countess's eyes widened in what

Susanna could only understand was mock horror.

"It is simple, darling Leonie, the only person I love and am ever likely to love, is you. You have done more for my happiness than anyone and tonight I want to repay you. Arleta has told me what you like, Leonie."

Leonie nodded her head ever so slightly – she put out a hand and very lightly squeezed Susanna's hand. "You know I want only your happiness but I cannot be with you for ever, Susanna, I have my husband. We have children…"

"It is enough that I *have* you, Leonie. And between your visits I have Arleta to keep me company. I shall be very content."

Leonie raised her fan, placing it over her lips. Her eyes travelled the room, they must appear as a very respectable pair, and almost she wanted to laugh out loud at the idea!

"I do love you, Susanna. I think I always have."

"I know," Susanna said. "You proved that by giving Arleta to me. You made me very happy and so, tonight, when these people have gone, I will make you happy too."

"And your parents very unhappy!"

"Ah yes, what they wished for me, I now wish for them. That is my gift to them."

The Gatecrasher
by Stephen Albrow

Curiosity might have killed the cat, but that wasn't enough to put Charlotte off. It wasn't easy climbing over the wall in six-inch heels and a rubber mini, but she ignored the 'Trespassers Will Be Prosecuted' sign and stepped onto the lush, green pasture. She could see the manor house up in the distance, at the end of a twisting pathway, which cut through the centre of the orchard. It was getting late and getting dark, but she couldn't see or hear any signs of revelry. Maybe the rumours weren't true, after all! Maybe the Lord just hated ramblers!

Nervous but excited, Charlotte headed for the pathway and started making her way to the manor house. The dispute and the rumours had been the talk of the village, ever since the new, young Lord had first put up the 'No Trespassing' sign. There was a covenant in the parish law book that guaranteed full right of way through the manor grounds. It had been written in 1352. None of the previous Lords had ever challenged its validity, but Richard Parker was a different beast altogether – much younger for a start, at 32, and someone perhaps with secrets to hide.

Charlotte had seen him on the local news just after he'd inherited the title from his father. She was struck by how good-looking he was, but there was something else about his face – he had a look of inbred authority about him, which allowed her to believe some of the wilder local gossip. People were saying he wanted to keep the ramblers and riffraff out so no one got to hear about the parties he liked to throw each weekend. What went on at these parties tended to differ depending on who you spoke to in the village. Some called them swinging sessions, others outright orgies, while a few talked of rubber, leather and chains and claimed to have heard desperate cries of pain.

Determined to find out for herself, and equally determined to meet the handsome Lord, Charlotte made her way through the orchard. There was a full moon in the sky that night, which cast shadows all around her, the branches of the apple trees forming a spider's web on the orchard floor. The creepiness unnerved her, as did the overpowering silence, which was broken only by the squeak of her rubber mini and the crunch of her heels on the gravel path. She could see the manor house getting nearer, but still there was no sign of life. Perhaps it was all a waste of time, but no, it couldn't be – she had seen that look in Richard Parker's eyes; his dominant twinkle, his superior shine!

Leaving the orchard behind her, Charlotte strode through the ornamental garden, with its gushing fountains and manicured lawns. There were no lights on in the manor house, so she took the path to the left of the building, which led to Richard Parker's outdoor pool. Her footsteps were getting smaller now. She was almost up on tiptoes, for fear of giving herself away. If a party was taking place that night, then it would be taking place just around the corner. Tentatively, she took another step closer and, bingo, she heard music. So something was going on that night!

Her heartbeat quickening, Charlotte leaned forward, ready to peek round the side of the house. The pool was still some fifty feet away, but already she could hear the splashes and screams of people messing about in the water. She was almost scared of looking, in case it turned out to be a huge disappointment. What if it was just a few friends larking around in a pool? Charlotte had tried not to appear overly interested when the villagers had gossiped about the orgiastic excesses going on at the manor. But the truth was the stories had excited her more than anything else before in her life.

Charlotte longed to be dominated by the handsome Lord of the Manor, hence the outfit she'd chosen to trespass in. Her breasts were made to look enormous by her highly restrictive push-up corset, while her rubber skirt barely covered her arse, exposing her highly spankable thighs. As soon as he saw her, the Lord would sense her deep, submissive desires, just as she had sensed his authoritarian manner the moment she'd seen him on TV. But first the rumours had to be true, and there was only one way of finding it!

Charlotte stepped round the corner, her pulse racing, as she feasted her eyes on a wall of bare flesh. A naked blonde dived into the pool, which was already filled with copulating couples, whose thrusting churned up the water's surface. It was an orgy, all right, but what about the more colourful talk of leather, chains and cries of pain? Charlotte hid behind a marble statue, then, peeking out, she spotted him. He wore a long, dark cloak and was carrying a whip. A pair of leather-clad twins stood one either side of him.

A tortured moan filled the night-time air, diverting Charlotte's attention to the far side of the pool. Her pussy pulsed, as she saw a young woman draped across another's lap. The second woman, dressed in a corset and brandishing a rubber baton, delivered six fierce blows to the younger girl's behind. Charlotte watched, transfixed, and then she turned to Richard Parker. He was watching just as eagerly, while fingering the shaft of his whip, as if impatient for the domme to strike the bad girl even harder.

Watching the young Lord caressing his whip made

Charlotte's pussy drip with juice. The domme's corset and baton had excited her, too, because it proved this was more than a swingers' night. Darker deeds were taking place here, but did she dare to get involved? She wondered what the young woman had done to incur such a painful act of retribution. But it can't have been any worse than trespassing, so Charlotte's punishment was sure to be even more extreme.

An icy shiver turned her flesh to goose-bumps, as another howl of anguish filled the air. The girl was having her hair pulled now. The domme was using it like a dog's lead, dragging the girl around the pool to face the wrath of Richard Parker. Charlotte heard the hum and lash of his whip, as he tested out his weapon on the poolside paving, the whiplash crack calling everyone to attention. All the sexed up couples and trios in the pool turned towards their Master, eager to see him putting his whip to use. Even Charlotte stepped forward, keen to get a better view of the tall, muscular nobleman chastising the girl.

No sooner had she taken the step, Charlotte was regretting it. She hadn't noticed the gun dogs lying in the corner, obediently watching over their Lord and Master. And the dogs hadn't noticed Charlotte either, but now she was firmly in their sights. Growling, barking and baring their fangs, they sprinted forth and surrounded her. They knew their job. It was to hold the intruder captive till their Master had stepped forward and declared her friend or foe.

With the dogs having made such a frightful sound, all eyes now turned to Charlotte. The other young submissive was spared a whipping, as Richard Parker went to see what his hounds had caught. His cloak trailing in the wind, he strode towards the gatecrasher, a leather-clad twin on either side. He called off the dogs, who fell silent and stopped jumping the very instant they heard his voice.

"So, what have we here?" asked Richard Parker, eyeing

up Charlotte's tempting body. His gaze lingered over her thighs and bottom, as if searching for the best bits to whip and spank.

"I'd heard about your parties," Charlotte whispered, her voice getting stuck in the back of her throat.

"I'd heard about your parties, *Master*," the dominant Lord corrected her, then he made her repeat her words again. She did so without question. He was not a man to argue with. Standing well over six feet tall, and with a whip in his hand, Richard Parker demanded total compliance!

"Well, I'm afraid you weren't invited," he said, making eye contact with Charlotte for the very first time. His piercing eyes seemed to see right through her, then just like that, he turned and walked away. It felt to Charlotte like the ultimate snub, but in fact it was just part of Richard Parker's game. As he marched back to the pool, he suddenly barked a command to his two female slaves, ordering them to grab the trespasser and bring her to the punishment zone.

Obeying their Master, the leather-clad twins both grabbed one of Charlotte's slender arms. She didn't know whether to fight with them, or just let them lead her over to the pool. In the end, she had no choice – though cute and pretty, the twins were surprisingly strong. Not only that, they were more than happy to manhandle Charlotte in order to fulfil their Master's wishes.

"Don't fight it or you'll just make him more angry," warned one of the duo, but Charlotte's instincts were telling her to run. Up ahead, she could see Richard Parker flailing his long, sharp whip through the air. The lengthy train danced around like a serpent, and with an equally vicious sting in its tail. And these were only practice strokes – the real ones were sure to hold much more venom.

"I'm scared," whispered Charlotte, who was mesmerised by the dancing whip.

"Well, don't be," said the second twin. "Trust in the Master. He knows best."

These words proved strangely comforting to Charlotte, as she was led over to be dealt with by Richard Parker. The partygoers in the water all turned to watch, as the new girl was forced down to her knees. The twins knelt beside her, still clutching her arms, then bowed their heads to their all-powerful Master.

"We don't like trespassers here," said Richard Parker, circling Charlotte's vulnerable body. "We don't like people who intrude on our parties uninvited, then gossip with the locals about the bad things going on at the manor."

"I'd never gossip-" Charlotte interjected.

"Silence when I'm speaking," shouted Richard Parker. "You really are a terrible girl." He was clearly enjoying his oratory. The people in the pool and his leather-clad slaves were hanging on his every word. As was Charlotte, whose fate was in the Lord and Master's whip-wielding hands.

"You are a terrible girl, who must be punished," he bellowed, pronouncing his judgment on the uninvited guest. A sickly sensation struck Charlotte's stomach, as Richard Parker then clicked his fingers at the twins. It seemed to be a practised routine, as one twin hitched up Charlotte's skirt and the second twin yanked her knickers down. They then forced Charlotte onto all fours, while Richard Parker waited behind her, making her feel more vulnerable than ever before in all her life.

Nevertheless, she couldn't wait for the moment when his whip would strike her for the very first time. For all the nervous jangling in her stomach, this was something she'd wanted for ages, so she closed her eyes and calmed herself, then waited for the thrilling burst of pain.

"Bad, bad girl," said Richard Parker, then his long, sleek whip thrashed through the air. Charlotte heard it first, then felt it second – a sharp and blistering burst of pain. Her face creased in agony and a groan burst from her lips, like the air spewing out of a bicycle puncture. Her buttocks were already starting to throb, just from the initial strike, and now she heard the rustle of the nobleman's cloak, as he raised his arm on high once more.

"You nasty bitch," said the formidable Master, lashing the whip into Charlotte's behind. This time she couldn't prevent herself from screaming, as the ferocious strike turned her arse cheeks red. The serpentine coil had struck both bare buttocks, before curling round her hip, then slithering back. And there was still more to come – straightaway she heard the chilling crack, as the whip flew high and then straightened out, delivering another burst of pain to her cheeks.

"No more," yelled Charlotte, unsure if she meant it, but certain of the mounting soreness in her arse. She longed to pull her knickers back up, to cushion just a fraction of the torturous pain, but something stopped her from reaching back. Was it the sticky wetness of her pussy, which seemed to increase with each new blow? Or was it, more specifically, that she wanted Richard Parker to smell her free-flowing sexual juices?

"You reek like a slut," he yelled on cue, as he executed another fierce lash. The coil unfurled and struck both buttocks, zinging through the air with a truly unforgiving zeal. Charlotte screamed, but Richard Parker still wanted more from her, so he ordered the twins to expose her breasts. Their delicate hands unfastened her corset, then she felt their fingers on her trembling mounds.

"Hurt her nipples," commanded Richard Parker, then three bursts of pain hit Charlotte at once. As the whip tore her aching arse to ribbons, the twins' long, scarlet fingernails started digging into her swollen teats. Manicured to razor-like sharpness, the nails were deadly weapons, as jagged and fierce as any nipple clamp. They dug deeper and deeper, while twisting the buds, both arousing and hurtful at the same time.

"Oh, god," groaned Charlotte, staring across the pool, where everyone was happily watching her punishment. Not that anyone seemed interested in Charlotte. Their eyes were all upon Richard Parker. Standing tall behind her, the Master raised his arm on high and trained a whiplash blow on Charlotte's pert rump. But it was almost too much. What with the mounting pain in Charlotte's nipples, the gatecrasher had been pushed just about as far as she was able to go.

Charlotte felt herself grow dizzy, as pain and arousal overwhelmed her mind. She didn't have a safe word, so she was grateful to have an intuitive Master. Sensing the young girl's limits had been reached, Richard Parker dropped down to his knees behind her.

"Have you learned your lesson?" he asked. There was a reassuring warmth in his voice.

"Yes, Master."

"Good. You took your lesson well. And the reward for withstanding pain is pleasure."

The switch was so sudden, it took a moment for Charlotte to readjust. The twins released their razor-like grip on her nipples, then took her sore teats within their mouths. At the same time, Richard Parker threw aside his whip, then from behind, he pressed his prick between her legs. She felt his hardness, as it slid inside her sticky gash, ramming into her just as forcefully as the whip had lashed into her arse.

Charlotte closed her eyes and smiled, as Richard Parker started thrusting. His rigid cock, made hard by the excitement of punishing her, powered in and out of her deep, wet orifice, sparking tingles of pleasure throughout her cleft. His hands were on her buttocks, gripping tight enough to remind her of the way she'd been disciplined with the whip. His fingertips dug into her sensitive flesh, agitating the sore spots, as he fucked her like the masterful man he was.

A wave of spasms shot through Charlotte's pussy, as she revelled in Richard Parker's sexual dominance. His dick surged to and fro inside her, making her scream after every thrust, while the two pretty twins added further pleasure, their mouths and tongues stimulating her nipples. It felt like an act of complete surrender. She had given her body over to the Master and his minions, first to punish and now to pleasure in any way that he saw fit. Luckily, the trust she'd placed in him was about to be repaid in full, as the pulsing throbs in her cock-filled pussy reached a near-orgasmic intensity.

With Charlotte's cunt spasming hard around his manhood, Richard Parker drew his pelvis back. His long, thick cock slid out of her body, with just his bulbous helmet remaining inside. The pre-orgasmic tension inside her gash had taken him to the verge of a climax, so he drove his phallus straight back home. His full-length thumped inside her body, the athletic force of the final thrust triggering fierce pulsations in his helmet, matching those in Charlotte's cunt.

Charlotte yelled, as a thick wave of spunk came gushing out of Richard Parker's head. His helmet was bulging in the depths of her orifice, the bulges sending shivers through her vaginal walls. She felt more of his jism spurt into her pussy – the proof that she had satisfied her Master – and then it was her turn to release her sexual spray. It seeped out of her orifice, the sticky fluid warming her thighs. And still his helmet throbbed inside her. And still the leather-clad twins sucked her teats.

As her orgasmic high reached a blissful zenith, Charlotte looked back at her powerful Master. Staring straight at her, he swung his hips again, the movement of his cock inside her pussy causing Charlotte's muscles to pulse and churn. Her heart was pumping at maximum speed now. The blood in her veins felt hot enough to burn. She could even feel her face flushing red, but not as red as her bare bottom. For the first time, she saw the whip marks on her cheeks. A smiling Richard Parker prodded each welt.

"These will remind you never to trespass again," he said, but Charlotte could see the twinkle in his eyes. Although he was reprimanding her, and reminding her of the lesson she'd been made to learn, she knew she'd never have to gatecrash another of Richard Parker's parties. His dick was still bulging inside her pussy, the continued force of his orgasmic pulsations leaving her in no doubt how satisfied he was with his new slave. From hereon in, she could expect to receive an invitation. By withstanding the pain and sharing the pleasure, she was now one of the gang.

All Right On The Night
by Jo Nation

Every Wednesday, Fenella goes to George Hawker's apartment taking the Number 42 bus through congested traffic sitting on the top deck looking out at shoppers dawdling by plate glass windows seeking custom, and the fleet of foot striding ahead of the traffic-snarled bus.

George Hawker's apartment is the most modern Fenella has ever seen, not that it's in a new building; that's its joy. The shell is a stone building five storeys high with a proud pediment proclaiming its Victorian heritage. The original works closed years back, the building lay idle for an age before developers moved in with an army of hard-hat, bare-chested young builders who swarmed over the building through a long, hot summer.

Fenella had often passed by *The Foundry,* as the apartments are now called, while the builders laboured. One baking day, her bus held up by a delivery van stood stationary as bronzed builders on the scaffolding only feet away looked in at her looking out and mouthed their kisses; she smiled, a butterfly stirred, a tingle flickering deep within, fermenting excitement. She pursed her lips in reply and held the tallest guy's eye. Hands moved to his tool-slung builders' belt, his thumbs hooking in to pull down on his waistband revealing pale skin and wisps of golden hair; he spread his fingers and played music on his jeans.

The traffic eased, the bus pulled away. Fenella looked back at the lads grinning from the scaffolding to meet the eye of a frowning elderly passenger glaring disapproval along the bus.

Apartment C2, on the far corner of *The Foundry* away from the bustle of traffic, looks out on gardens laid over the old foundry yard. Solid timber floors in the reception rooms are spread with Mid-Eastern carpets, a marble clad en-suite wet room and a kitchen of stainless steel fittings with Italian tiling complete the transformation that has been worked in the once industrial building. The apartment – cool in summer and warm in winter – is the epitome of young couple style with a keypad code to access the building, another to gain entry to the apartment.

The luxury of Apartment C2 is in stark contrast to the flat Fenella and Julian call home, undecorated for years with a broken window on their communal landing. It's adequate for their needs, not that Julian ever sees much of the place; he works too hard, spending long hours into the night and back to his City desk for the European markets' morning opening. Julian disapproves of Fenella's reluctance to take on what he calls a proper job; she senses it's his excuse knowing his interest is cooling; the fun is gone from their romance. If only they could spend time together, get away to a place in the sun.

Fenella's great envy at Apartment C2 is the en-suite to the master bedroom, the power-shower is to die for, its pulsing needle massage foaming lavender shower cream is the high point of her every visit. If only she could lure Julian to the apartment, her ultimate excitement in the wet room would be to share its pulsating rhythm with him. After showering she gives the tiled room a clean, the only strenuous housework she does for George. Not bothering to dress, she works naked until her task is finished and it's time to put on her tee shirt, jeans and trainers to head home.

Fenella has never met George Hawker, nor even spoken with him by telephone; she was recommended by one of her other cleaning clients with everything arranged by letter, her best break since the dreaded summons to the manager's office at the building society with the stark redundancy Form P45 handed across the table. Working for George is undemanding and well paid, even by the standards of the leafy London suburbs.

Most evenings with no Julian at the flat Fenella makes herself useful backstage at the local theatre; it's unpaid labour, but she dreams one day she'll be taking her cue and walking onto the boards as the curtain rises.

Her duties at Apartment C2, or Fenella's interpretation of them, are simple: tidy and clean the already neat rooms, hardly disturbed since her last visit. So she fills her time with a lingering coffee drunk from the kitchen's art deco cups before flicking a duster around the furniture. Then, her token cleaning done, it's off to the en-suite to strip and luxuriate in the massaging shower before posing in front of the cheval mirror, every inch of her nakedness available for inspection.

Fenella likes the body she sees, her breasts rounded and firm, her nipples pink and excited as she fingers her sex wondering if she should shave the silky tress of her pubes. Would Julian notice if she did?

Fenella is puzzled; she knows there are things that don't add up about Apartment C2 and its owner George Hawker. No family photos decorate the spacious lounge, there is never any sign other people visit the apartment, indeed there's scant evidence of George's existence. The place is a magazine-spread of minimalist living.

George Hawker's closet off the master bedroom is the

sole secret place at Apartment C2; drawers, the scarcely used wardrobes, kitchen units and the larder; Fenella looks through them all on every visit hoping to learn something about her employer. The locked closet frustrates her. There has to be a spare key secreted at the apartment somewhere.

To spur her curiosity Fenella vetoes her usual indulgence in the wet room until the closet is unlocked be it today, next week, or whenever. The lure of the shower massaging her body, the thrill of the handheld showerhead pulsating between her thighs bringing ecstasy to climax threatens her vow even as she makes it. How can she wait another week, even another hour?

But there is no key to the closet.

She tries drawers in the bedroom and the kitchen, feels along edges in the decor, lifts potted plants, but all to no avail, her search is fruitless; there is no key.

In a desperate bid, Fenella puts her shoulder to the closet door, turns the oft-tried doorknob, and overbalances into the void.

The frustration of her search evaporates as wide-eyed she explores shelves and clothes racks so suddenly revealed within the small room.

How come the closet is unlocked today?

There are leather suits in women's styles, lingerie, DVDs, explicit books and, hooked over a rail, a collection of canes of varying size, schoolmaster's canes with curled handles. There are pairs of fine leather gloves, masks, belts, ropes and a tawse, its split leather ends cut into many tails. George's secrets are there to behold. Fenella thumbs the pages of a slim volume, a tale of a Victorian chambermaid stealing her Ladyship's jewellery forced to take stern consequence from his Lordship. Tinted line drawings show the maid's glowing buttocks, but the smile of her full-lipped glance, and the look of pleasure on the Lord's face with his breeches round his knees, indicates the punishment is not quite what her Ladyship intended.

The closet's secrets champion deep stirrings; Fenella needs to share its excitement imagining George tall, dark and commanding standing in front of her, his eyes scanning her willing body submitting to his punishment. But why the neatly folded lingerie on the shelves, the female-wear hanging on the rails? Would she be dressed in this finery to kneel as supplicant before George? Could she lure Julian to Apartment C2 to share the bounty she had found?

A window from floor to ceiling in the en-suite wet room with thin curtains draped across looks out over the garden; Fenella pulls them back, opening the window; she wants no barrier between her showering nakedness and the outside world. Her body responds to her daring, her flesh tingles priming her nipples to stand hard and proud. She shuts her eyes wanting to be seen her glistening body lit by ceiling spotlights, wanting a stranger, the young man working in the gardens to watch from his distance, wanting to take her.

'What the hell is going on here?'

Fenella gulps a mouthful of foaming water and gags; she stares wet-eyed at the tall figure in the doorway of the master bedroom.

'Well?'

'What are you doing in here?' Fenella's voice cracks. She tries to clear her throat, excitement tingling deep within as the intruder's eyes explore her exposed flesh dripping in the shower.

'Never mind me. What are you doing in the shower?'

'This is Mr George Hawker's apartment, and I work here.'

'I see. Perhaps you won't work here much longer. Let me introduce myself. I'm Georgina Hawker. My friends call me George.'

How has she never realised Apartment C2 isn't a man's

lair? The tall woman is wearing a black suit of a finely cut three quarter length jacket, tailored trousers to her calf and exquisite wedged sandals laced to her ankles with red bindings and hints of crimson nail varnish.

There's something familiar in the woman's style and her voice.

'I'm Fenella. I'm sorry you've found me in the shower; I spilt cleaning fluid and had to wash it off. I meant no harm.'

'It isn't the first time you've had shower here, is it?'

Chill seeped in after the hot pounding of the massaging shower.

'And you drink my coffee; you don't clean the place. I'll be better off without you.'

Fenella's heart sinks, only evening bar work could make up for George's wages, there'd be no time to work backstage at the theatre. Then it clicks. This woman is Mrs Everson, the power behind the Civic Theatre Trust.

'I promise it won't happen again.'

'It's happened too many times already.'

'Please, Ms Hawker, don't sack me, I need this job. If I have done wrong, punish me.' Fenella blushes; memories of the Nun she'd worshipped at convent school, the Nun who'd called her up to the front of class, pulled up her skirt and stung the back of her thighs with a ruler, it all floods back. She hangs her head not believing the rash words she'd spoken.

'You've been prying into my closet, you wretched girl. Have you forced the lock?' The women look at each other, their breath tightening, both knowing the urge to go further.

'It was open.'

Without a word George reaches out, grips Fenella's nipple between her forefinger and thumb, plays with it until it's erect in her grasp and presses, pinching harder as she looks Fenella in the eye. 'You're a liar. Dry yourself, get a bathrobe and come through to the sitting room. I'll decide what to do with you.' George turns and strides from the room.

Alone, Fenella crouches on the WC, easing her sore breast. She could grab her trainers and clothes from the bed and might get away, but there would be no job.

Her clothes have gone, there's only a bathrobe on the bed; you can't catch a bus in a bathrobe.

In the sitting room stripped of her suit, her raven hair let down to reach her shoulders, George stands tall, her feet apart wearing thigh boots, lace-edged scarlet French knickers with her breasts eager under a matching camisole. In her gloved hands, she grasps a hooked cane from the rail in the closet; gas flames lick over beach stones in the fireplace. Fenella can't stifle the tears rolling down her cheeks.

'Don't snivel, girl. Take your punishment and you can keep your job, but only on probation. Come here, kneel and tell me what wrong you have committed.'

Fenella kneels, her face close to George, sensing the musk of her body, trembling at the expectation of her punishment. George holds out her gloved hand to Fenella's face.

'Kiss my hand.'

Fenella's lips quiver on the fine calfskin; there is a ring under the leather.

'Take off my glove, then kiss my palm.'

With shaking fingers Fenella eases the fitted glove from George's hand. When her lips brush the cool palm George slides her hands through Fenella's hair to pull her face onto her belly.

'Take off your robe and say thank you for what you are about to receive.'

'Thank you, George.'

'And?'

'For what I am about to receive.'

Naked, Fenella is led to a high-backed chair to bend over the arm. The ringed hand spanks down after a calculated pause. Fenella stiffens with the shock of it, the sting on her buttock like burning water. The second and third come on alternate buttocks, George's free hand firmly holding the nape of her neck. The stinging hand comes again, and again, reddening Fenella's backside as she squirms pressing herself onto the chair.

'Now that I have warmed you up, say 'Thank you', and count each spank I give you. I shall decide how many you will have.' George's hand caresses Fenella's glowing fundament, soothing her anxiety, kindling exhilaration as she pushes her backside up from the chair to meet the speeding hand.

'One, thank you, Ms Hawker.' Fenella waits for the hand to come down again. 'Two, thank you, Mrs Everson.'

There is silence in the room.

'You impudent spying wretch, you've asked for it. It will be the cane now. Get back over the chair.'

Fenella grips the leather cushion fearing her nails will break as six strokes of the cane, each counted and thanked in her small voice, distress her backside, the swish of the cane heralding each stroke, each harder than its precursor stinging her rounded cheeks.

'Don't ever call me Mrs Everson again.'

'I won't, George. I promise.'

On the large bed, the two women hug each other; George kisses the tears from Fenella's eyes and gently strokes her roasted buttocks.

Now Fenella understands why the closet had been locked on earlier days, and why it is now unlocked on the day George planned to surprise her. She was meant to find it open. She kisses George's breast, taking the dark nipple in her lips and tongues it to excitement, she lets her hair stroke down George's torso, nuzzles her abdomen before she eases her employer's legs apart and tastes her moist unseen lips, the tangy ooze waking her tongue. Fenella has known her own vagina, explored its mystery with her hand, building lonesome excitement with wet fingers sliding into her own warmth; now she pushes her tongue deep into another's place and loves her.

'Was I cruel to you?'

'I thought I would get away with it.'

'Then I caught you red handed.'

'Red backside, more like; can I keep coming to clean for you, George?'

George eases her jewelled ring from her finger, kisses it and places it in Fenella's hand. 'Take this as a memento of the day.'

'George, it's beautiful.'

'Fenella, I want you to come to one of my evening parties; it's not only girls, it's men and women. Would you like that?'

'You mean here at the apartment? I thought no one ever came here.'

'It may surprise you to know I clean up after every party; you'll be able to help me. You'll enjoy meeting my chums; don't be misled by this afternoon. We all have fun together.'

'Is it only couples?'

'Oh no, my husband Max would never understand my parties. He knows nothing about them. I run my own business; Apartment C2 is on the company books for entertainment purposes. You can bring your partner if you want.'

'Julian, I doubt he's ready for this, not yet.'

'I might fancy him.'

'That's the problem; he's got a wandering eye. When is your party?'

'Friday evening; you'll be in your element.'

'Friday is rehearsal night at the theatre.'

'That's where I first saw you, at a Theatre Trust reception.'

'I only work backstage.'

'You'll be front stage here. You'll be the star in the night's charades.'

'What?'

'At every party we first play out a scenario on a theme of my choosing. It'll be your acting challenge, the stage will be yours.'

'Oh, my God; is it dressy?'

'Smart and sexy, but you might not be wearing your costume for too long.' George gives Fenella a pat on her still red backside. 'My business interests include *Can She Can*, the boutique in the new Central Mall selling provocative wear to exciting people. I'll give you free rein to get kitted out at the shop. We'll make you the Belle of the Ball.'

Fenella unlatches the door of her flat, steps into darkness running her hand along the familiar wall to find the light switch. Is Julian at home? She wants Julian; she needs to satisfy a man.

She is alone.

In her bed she falls asleep dreaming of George's *Puritans and Pirates Party*. George has promised her the lead on Friday night, maybe not the scenario you would put onto a public stage, but who knows? The great stars all had to start somewhere. It's too absurd. She laughs pulling the duvet over her head.

'What's the joke?'

Julian is in bed beside her. 'Did I laugh? I was dreaming,

darling.' In the depth of the night he is strong and overwhelming, the hard centre of her sweet confection.

Fairground Attraction
by Mimi Elise

The lights from the fairground beckoned me closer. I told myself I was too old for such things, but a visit that afternoon with some younger family members reminded me how much fun was to be had at the fair.

I'd been encouraged – teased – into going in and seeing the fortune-teller. I always laughed at such things and waited for her to tell me I'd meet a tall, dark, handsome stranger. She was quite handsome herself. Beautiful really, with long raven hair, and a gypsy top that revealed perfect shoulders and the tantalising hint of cleavage. I've never been with a woman, but I found myself getting aroused when she took my hand in hers, stroking my hand from wrist to fingertip with long, cool fingers. It sent a shiver down my spine, and as I looked at her full, sensual mouth, I wondered what it would be like to kiss her and slip my tongue between those lips.

"I see you having lots of fun at the fairground," she told me. "And lots of rides."

"What? No tall, dark, handsome stranger?"

"Tall, dark, blond, handsome, rugged. Why just settle for one man when you can have one, two, three…?"

I wriggled in my seat a little, feeling the heat rising in my sex. Surely fortune-telling wasn't supposed to go like this. She'd just described one of my favourite fantasies, where several men pleasure me. I was both intrigued and bothered that she knew so much about me.

"Come back later," she said, in a silky voice. "Much later."

From the moment I left the tent, I was acutely aware of every man at the fairground. The barker on the carousel, who I was sure brushed my bum as he helped me onto a horse; the guy who operated the ghost train, who pressed his hand against my wrist as he assisted me into the cart; the man on the waltzer who stopped me from falling as I tumbled off, cupping my breast in his hand, seemingly by accident. It was as if they all knew me, and were part of some conspiracy to heighten my senses and make me want what the fortune-teller promised.

So I went back much later, as she'd suggested. I passed young couples wandering home to finish what they'd started in the Tunnel of Love.

"We're closing up," said an old fella, who was sweeping away the debris of the day. I ignored him. He wasn't going to feature in my fantasy. He shrugged and went off to his caravan, muttering something about 'She's at it again, I see'.

They were waiting for me at the carousel. Three men. One dark, one fair, and one somewhere in between. They were all tall and beautiful, with tans that can only be achieved by spending all day in the open air. One was carrying a piece of black cloth.

"You can stop this any time you want," he said, moving towards me. I realised it was a blindfold, and my stomach lurched a little, because the fortune-teller had seen that part of my fantasy too. "Just say stop and we will."

I nodded my understanding, unable to speak because of the excitement caught in my throat. A few seconds later I was blindfolded. I felt his hand stroke my bare shoulder. "Ready?" he whispered against my ear. I nodded again.

Hands caught my arms and guided me up the steps of the carousel, catching me when I stumbled a little. Unseen hands switched on the machine and the carousel began to turn slowly. The hands holding me began to remove my clothing; my skimpy vest top, my short skirt and my shoes. At that point, none of them had touched me sexually, and yet the brush of hands against my thighs, against my belly, aroused me immensely. I tried to guess which hands did what, but gave up. The confusion was far too enjoyable.

Suddenly I was hoisted up to sit on the back of one of the horses, my hot sex pressing against the cool metal. Within seconds someone sat behind me. He was naked too, and I felt his hardening cock press against the small of my back. His hands trailed around the front of my body, stroking me, tweaking my nipples, then sliding down to my sex, whilst his lips traced gentle kisses along my shoulders. My sex throbbed with longing, and I could feel the metal beneath me becoming wetter as his fingertip rolled my clit. All the time, the carousel was moving up and down, shifting his cock against my back as it did, sliding it between the cheeks of my ass. The sensation was both pleasurable and strange to me.

"Stand up," he ordered. I did as I was told, feeling his fingers come at me from behind, delving deep into my vagina. The rhythm of the carousel caused his fingers to slide in and out. I could barely hold onto the pole, my body was trembling so much. I felt his hands on my hips. I leaned forward a little, then pushed my ass out towards him. He eased me down onto his hard cock. I didn't need the carousel to set the rhythm then. I worked against it, grinding down onto him, wanting him deeper and deeper inside me. I could feel my belly tighten as an orgasm began to burn in my groin. He was slamming into me, losing the control that he'd worked so hard to maintain. It aroused me even more. I wanted to be the best fuck he'd ever had. I tightened the muscles in my vagina, causing him to cry out as I gripped, released, gripped, released. I came just before he did, collapsing against the pole in ecstasy.

Before I could recover, hands were upon me again, taking me from the carousel. They carried me I knew not where. Finally, I was settled in a cart somewhere, and one of the men got in beside me. Again, unseen hands started the ride. I guessed, by the faint sounds within, that it was the ghost train. When the cart moved, lips covered mine, and a tongue delved into my mouth. I returned the kiss hungrily. His kisses trailed down my body, and I felt him move so that he was kneeling in the narrow leg space of the cart. His hands touched my thighs, pinching them slightly, then opening them, so I could imagine him look directly at my sex. His tongue found my throbbing clit, then his teeth nibbled at it lightly. He ran his tongue the full length of me, again and again, lapping up the moisture left from my previous encounter. The idea of him tasting it all turned me on even more. I pushed myself against his mouth, begging him to taste all. Meanwhile, disembodied screams filled the air, but they weren't as loud as my own screams when he brought me to an orgasm just in time for the cart to reach the open air again.

I guessed where they were going to carry me next, but I had no idea how this was going to work. One of the men sat beside me whilst the others secured us into the seat.

"What now?" I said.

"Suck me," he said. I was glad. I'd loved every minute of it so far, but I wanted to feel and taste one of them for a change. To make this experience more real.

I reached out to touch him, to try and get my bearings, whilst the machine started up. My hands found a firm chest and tight belly, then his hard cock bobbed near to my hand. I leaned down, guided by his hand and took him in my mouth. He groaned, as the waltzer spun more and more. I felt his cock touch the back of my throat as it spun, and at one point it slipped from my mouth. But I kept hold of him with my hands, and continued sucking him hard, feeling his body tense beneath me, while the machine spun and spun. He was twitching, trying to stop himself from coming, but one especially fast spin threw him off guard, and he came in my mouth. I lapped him up hungrily.

When the waltzer stopped, I wondered what would happen next. I'd used up all the rides. Strong arms hoisted me up, so I was in a sitting position. They walked for some time and I sensed I was being taken away from the rides, to some other location.

A few minutes later, I was lying on a soft bed. The blindfold had been removed, so I could see my lovers. I could see the shadow of someone sitting in the corner, and I knew she was watching us, so I pulled the nearest man down to me, kissing him full on the mouth. The blond was licking my thighs, and the darker man sucked my nipples. Their hands were everywhere.

"I want all of you to fuck me," I said. "Show her what you can do to please a woman."

The blond got between my legs and hoisted my hips high. He pulled the lips of my sex apart, then thrust into me hard, pounding against me whilst the others covered my body in hot kisses, letting their tongues taste every inch of me. I reached out and touched them too, all my wonderful lovers. I came almost immediately, overwhelmed by the sensuality of it all.

The dark man was going to take the blond's place, but I sat up and flipped him over, straddling his thighs. I reached down and kissed his mouth, then eased myself down onto his cock.

"Is this arousing you?" I said to her. "Are you touching yourself?" I imagined her long fingernails biting into her sex, as she fought the excitement she must surely feel. Then

I imagined them biting into my sex.

To my surprise she moved towards the bed. In her hands was a small bowl. She sat on the edge of the bed, then leaned over and kissed me. "There's one pleasure you haven't known yet," she said. She dipped her fingers into the bowl and I saw that it contained oil. The third man sat behind me as I straddled his friend, and pulled my ass cheeks apart. I felt her fingers slide between them, and she pressed the warm oil against my anus.

"You can stop any time," she said, repeating what the men had said earlier. All the time her fingers were soaking the oil into my anus, and she slipped one finger inside me, to spread it further. I almost did stop her. I'd never done this before, but the excitement of the night and the moment overtook me. I wanted this. I wanted every sensation she and the men could offer me.

"I want it."

The man moved nearer still to me, and held me in place as he slipped his cock into my ass. It hurt at first, and I almost said stop, but other sensations took over. With the man beneath me, I felt as though I was completely full. They ground against me, tearing at me, yet making me feel as though I would explode with pleasure. The feeling was so intense, that when I came, I collapsed onto the bed, sure I was going to faint.

"Good girl," I heard her say, as she stroked my sweat-soaked hair. She muttered something to the men and they left. "You're such a good girl. Now, are you going to thank me?"

I thought I'd have nothing left in me, but when her red lips found mine, I felt myself becoming aroused again. We lay together, exploring each other's bodies. Touching her was like touching myself and I instinctively knew how to please her; licking her full, heavy breasts, pressing my tongue against her clit. I slid my fingers between her legs, fucking her with my fingers and tongue her until her body arched and she came in a rush against my mouth. Smiling, I licked my fingers, then put them in her mouth so she could taste it too. She smiled, running her tongue the length of my hands.

Sometime in the night, I awoke to feel her licking me, bringing me to one last, luxurious orgasm. When I awoke in the morning, the fairground was gone. I lay, naked in an empty field, with my clothes nearby; exhausted but very happy. I didn't know if it was all a dream, or whether I really had enjoyed a fairground attraction. I did know that the next time the fair was in town, I'd be the first in the queue!

Rodeo Girl
by Matt Pascoe

What am I doing? I must have been insane to agree to this. This is not who I am. Standing backstage my palms are sweaty and my heart is racing like a freight train. I think I'm actually having palpitations. What if I die? It could happen and then what? The medics find me dressed like this? There is a full length mirror just out of my eye-line. I take a step back and check myself out. Slim, some would say petite, five-foot seven inches, long brown hair and eyes to match. Chill out, girl! You look good. But I'm dressed in the skimpiest cowgirl outfit ever and it's riding right up my bum! What am I doing here? I must have been mad to agree to this.

Okay. So we've all thought about. We've all dreamed about it in our most day-dreamy of moments, in our darkest, super-slut sex-fuelled fantasies, but very few of us actually consider in the cold light of day dressing in our most skimpy, cleavage-skimming lingerie and shaking it for Joe Public and his good buddies. What the hell am I doing here standing in this boys' own club? I believe I am completely delusional. Someone please lock me up and throw away the key. I do not do this sort of thing. I am an office girl. My name is Penny. I work in accounts. I am such a good girl really.

"Hey, sugar!" She is blonde and beautiful and oh-so

curvy; a walking, talking, living, breathing Barbie Doll. "How are you doing?" Her stage name is Candy Cane.

"Not so good. I don't think I can do this."

"That's what we all think the first time, but really, it's not that bad. And it'll be over in a blink of an eye."

"What if I make a fool of myself? What if I fall over? That would look really great. I'd never be able to live it down."

"But dancing semi-naked is completely okay?"

"You're right. I have to get out of here right now. This was such a bad idea."

"You really are freaking out!" admits Candy.

"No shit, Sherlock!"

"Extreme circumstances require extreme measures. Come with me, missy!"

"Where are we going?" My resolve and nerves are crumbling by the second.

"To fix you up a rescue remedy; all the girls swear by it."

She takes me by the hand leading me through the backstage area, past feather boas and row upon row of leather costumes, guiding me into the changing room Candy Cane shares with four other senior dancers.

"Sit yourself down there and don't you worry about a thing. It's all going to be fine!"

"I wish I could believe you."

"Have a little faith, Rodeo Girl!"

With the deft touch of a seasoned bar pro, Candy mixes up a jug of some mysterious looking cocktail, that by the looks of the ingredients, is loaded and lethal. Locating two cocktail glasses she pours out two hefty measures filling the glasses to the rim.

"Drink it down, sugar." Clinking glasses, Candy sinks her measure and waits for me to do the same before pouring another.

"Getting me loaded is your great plan?"

"We're just taking the edge off to allow you to explore your creativity."

"That's a novel way of putting it."

"Stick with me, girl! I am the Queen of Creativity."

"Why do you do this and don't just say for the money?"

"The tips are good. You can't argue with that."

"But undressing in front of all those strangers? I don't think I can get my head around it."

"Stripping for strangers is a whole lot easier than getting your kit off in front of friends, though I've never really had an issue with it. I'm something of a show-off!"

"I'm not, though. When we met up at that Friends' Reunited meal you made it sound so easy, but I'm having such major butterflies here."

"Keep drinking!"

"I'll fall off the stage."

"Okay." Candy takes my glass from me. "You think about the money. You think of all the pretty things you're going to buy. You imagine the audience naked, though, that never really works for me because I just laugh. Or, you accept, that you're sexy as hell and you get off on the fact that these guys are sitting there getting horny over you. They all want to fuck you and they can't! For them, you are the ultimate object of desirability and you're completely out of reach. You're a good looking girl so why should you hide what God's given you. Why not make a few extra bucks from the fact that you're gorgeous. Sex sells, it always has and it always will."

"Amen to that!"

Candy's eyes light up. "Maybe there is hope for you?"

"When do I go on?"

"I asked the Chief to stall your opening night performance. There are a few things we need to iron out."

"You make it sound like it's no big deal?"

"It's not," assures Candy. "It's all just a state of mind."

"My state of mind is bordering on extreme terror!"

She leans across and kisses me full on the lips. I am so shocked that I don't react. I just freeze, motionless, lips not moving nor engaging, until Candy breaks free. She laughs at the fear written all across my face. "Don't look so worried, honey! I'm not trying to sleep with you. I'm just trying to loosen you up. When you get out there you have to make your audience believe that you are the sexiest thing to walk the Earth. Every single person sitting out there should be desperate to sleep with you."

"You're including women as well?"

"Women, animals, birds…you name it!"

"You're so funny!"

Candy pours another shot. We clink glasses and sink them. "Now for a little private education, Candy style! Stand up."

Pushing her chair aside, she turns on the black ipod nestling in the Bose speakers next to the row of mirrors, selects an R n' B track, and then seats herself on my chair.

"Okay, Rodeo Girl! I've just paid for a private lap dance. Now make me moist!"

"Just like that, you want me to turn it on?"

"That's the nature of the beast, sugar. Get your head straight and get into the mood. Make me wet for you!"

I close my eyes letting the rhythm flow through me. I start to sway, opening my eyes focusing on Candy, sitting there dressed in a tiny pink bikini, her voluptuous breasts straining to break free from the slivers of pink fabric holding them in place. Her blue eyes blaze with mischievousness but she remains motionless watching me sway before her.

"Closer." She mouths the words, her full cherry-red lips playing with the words and the strangest sensation comes over me. Is it the heat in the room, or is it me? A burning ache ignites deep inside me. She is so hot and I want her.

I sway in nearer, slower, grinding my hips, the distance between us closing so that the tips of my breasts brush hers. The feeling is electric. My nerve endings sizzle. It is like a drug coursing through my veins. I have never felt more alive than in this moment; right here and right now. I bite my lip and turn away backing into Candy's groin grinding down onto her, body heat rising.

Hands close on my breasts. Her breath is hot against my skin. Her lips are moist and sensuous, teasing, touching the nape of my neck. My nipples are hot to her touch, straining through the fabric of my own bikini top. I grind harder, deeper as her hands begin to slide, tracing the contours of my stomach going lower massaging my leather-clad thighs. I lean back turning my head to meet hers, lips seeking out lips, talking without making a sound. Her tongue eases into my mouth. We joust playfully as her fingers creep back up my thighs reaching the limits of my chaps, touching my bikini burrowing under.

I gasp, eyes open as her fingers enter me. I am so wet for her and it is all so new and strange. I have never slept with another woman, never wanted to, not even in my wildest of fantasies, but this just feels perfect. Her fingers push deeper in as I begin to rock against them. Harder, faster, just blissful! The urge builds like a wave of pleasure churning up the ocean, but I am greedy and I don't want it to end.

"Wait!" I take her hand drawing it back, easing off her, separating our horny bodies, facing her, the hunter and the hunted; our roles about to be reversed. My fingers intertwine with hers as I draw her from the chair backing her up against the wall of mirrors seeking out those cherry-red lips, delving in deeper, pushing her back, further back as we kiss; long, hard, passionate, kisses to be proud of. Candy eases herself up onto the polished surface wrapping her lithe limbs around my waist reaching round to untie the straps to her bikini as my mouth closes on her nipple, peeling the fabric away, chewing, tasting, licking, teasing and her pleasure is all my doing.

Candy leans back as her bikini top falls away and sighs. I leave a trail of kisses from her breasts all the way down to her belly.

"Lower!" Her voice is gruff with desire now and all bets are off. She leans away from me, arching her back pushing her groin further into me. I feel the smoothness of her honey limbs caressing them with my finger tips, the palm of my hand brushing over my bikini bottoms, her crotch warm and welcoming. Without hesitating I peel the flimsy fabric away dragging it down her thighs revealing her nakedness. Kicking the bottoms free I tease my fingers up her thighs, drawing circles going higher until they find her, hot and wet. She murmurs, she moans, I push deeper exploring her inner beauty. I taste her. She shudders. My tongue probes further. She screams! Candy writhes against me as I find a rhythm. For a beginner's effort, I am pleased.

Breaking for air Candy draws me up kissing me with abandon.

"Time to break out reinforcements," she whispers with unadulterated glee in her eyes. The rabbit sits silently in the make-up cabinet minding his own business. He buzzes to life as I back her into a corner raining kisses down on her. She has nowhere to go. The rabbit cuddles up to my thighs. My chaps fall away. Candy strips me naked; no discussion and no opposition. The rabbit burrows between my thighs, the pleasure sensation is white-hot. It obeys her every touch. She is a Jedi Master.

We clear the room, cosmetic products hitting the stratosphere in every direction. Her tongue devours my nipples. It is all a blur. She goes down on me, the pair of us lying amidst a heap of clothes on the dressing room floor. The sex is out of control. The rabbit hits warp speed. The

Duracell bunny has nothing on this rabbit!

Limbs entwined, bodies awash with sweat, the pounding of our hearts fills the silence. Candy props herself up on one elbow, pushing her messed up blonde hair out of her face, and studies me.

"You know, I think you've got the idea?"

"You do?"

"Yeah. You're going to fit in fine around here. The punters, they're going to love you. That's lesson number one, done and dusted! "

"That's good news."

"Are you ready for lesson number two?" Her eyebrows raised, the mischievousness is back!

"Just give me a minute, will you? I'm feeling a little hot and flustered."

"I can't think why?"

"No. Me either!"

"Okay. Well, give me a shout when you're ready."

"Okay." I lie back and close my eyes and let my heart rate settle. "This lap dancing business, I don't think it's going to be quite so hard after all!"

The Boss
by DMW Carol

He walks past me so many times during the day, or should I say struts. Everything about him screams alpha male from the way he thrusts his chest out ahead of him to the swagger in his hips. He knows he is the man. The boss. And God help any who forget it.

He issues his orders without thinking, arrogant tones echoing round the office. I wonder how much of the attitude is because he enjoys seeing the junior staff cringe and cower in front of him, hardly daring to report any issues in case they provoke his legendary temper.

He has never liked me, never trusted me, because I do not bow unquestioning to his male superiority. I smile as he sneers, I stand tall like he does and the sway in my hips is the same sway that woman has used to bring man to his knees since time began. He may rule the office, but he will never rule me.

One of these days I will show him. I will join the testosterone-fuelled throng headed to the pub on a Friday night. I will glide through their midst watching them relax, sharing their jokes, melding with the pack. I will smile and laugh and sway and he will know that in this place is it me who matters, not him.

It is not just him who can use a walk to demonstrate power. I will hold his eyes captive with every sway, brush close whenever there is an excuse and, as the incident caresses become longer and more obvious, I will allow him to feel that he has drawn my interest while I am snaring him in a web of sexual promise.

Gradually the others will depart, returning to families and a weekend of domestic bliss, but he will stay, held captive as the group grows ever more intimate. I will keep his attention firmly on the temptations I can offer and not allow his thoughts to stray to the mundane obligations that could lure him home. He will know that he and he alone is the focus of my lust that night, he will swell with pride and feel almost God-like. When we are finally alone he will think he has won, believe he has seduced me, but he will be wrong.

This will be no night for routine, so when the time comes I will lead him back to the office, to his own domain, to the sturdy desk that dominates the room and the soft leather couch where he invites his victims to relax before he strikes. Tonight he is my victim and it is him who sinks into the couch while I give him the first clue that this is my plan, not his, by producing the drinks and snacks I will have left in the office fridge earlier that day. I doubt he will feel anything but smug as I arrange music and glasses of chilled crisp white wine.

I hand him his drink and begin to dance as a track I like begins to play. I feel the music pounding through me, racing as fast as my pulse as I think of what I have planned. There is no room here for inhibition and I do not hold back, swaying and twirling with giddy abandon and keeping his eyes pinned on me. He cannot resist and I hear his breathing deepen as he watches me. His jacket is discarded and when he loosens his tie I know he is ready. I dance till the song ends anyway then laugh and relax as though I need to catch my breath.

As the music changes to something slower and more

earthy, I perch on the desk directly in front of him. I lean back to reach for my drink and let my legs splay slightly apart so he can glimpse the tops of my stockings under my skirt. One hand falls to my lap, ruffling the skirt to reveal a little more, just in case he hadn't noticed. I laugh as I see his gaze is exactly where I want it, and reach up to undo a couple of buttons on my shirt.

His husky groan tells me I have his full attention and the way he shifts in his seat signals that his arousal is becoming uncomfortably apparent.

"Take your shirt off," I command and without hesitation he complies. His physique is better than I imagined, well-defined muscles earned by many hours on the squash court, smooth unblemished skin with a smattering of dark hair curling across his chest. My tongue runs across the ends of my teeth, imagining it is tracing patterns across his chest, but I resist and settle instead for opening my own shirt and pulling it free of my skirt, letting it hang loose to reveal the fine lace half-cup bra beneath.

His gaze is drawn to my breasts and naturally they respond, nipples thrusting forward to welcome his attention. I let one hand follow his gaze, fingertip circling the aureole and easing the nipple above the lace. I dip one finger into the wine and return it to the caress leaving the nipple glistening and irresistible.

He tries to stand but I stop him in his tracks with a wave of my hand and the order to stay where he is. He is told to remove the rest of his clothes and sit back down and eagerly he complies.

He sits tall on the sofa, legs apart, cock standing to attention. He looks every inch the proud alpha male, but now we both know that I am the one controlling this scenario and while he thinks he knows what is coming, it will be on my terms not his.

I slide from the table and dance some more, allowing the

shirt to fall to the floor shortly followed by my skirt and knickers. As I expected his hand has reached for his cock and is beginning to stroke slowly along its length.

I turn so he can see I am watching him and his grip tightens. "Show me," I command and his caresses grow stronger and faster. I sink to my knees in front of him, eyes level with his rapidly moving hand. I lean back so he can watch my fingers slowly circling my clit, echoing his own caresses. He is moving almost in slow motion, trying to put on a good show, his gesture are languid and deliberate, curling around his length in a steady spiral running from head to base and then slowly retreating. The tension in his forearms reveals how hard he his fighting the temptation to go faster, afraid to seem too eager and end the moment too soon. His grip is tight enough to choke as it continues its path, covering every millimetre of his still-swelling cock.

"Come for me," I tell him, breaking his resistance and almost immediately his cock spits its load onto his stomach, thick white streaks against his glistening tanned skin. His groan is the primeval sound of total surrender and the spasm that shakes his body proves he is now as powerless as a kitten. Mine to command.

I lean forward and plant a kiss on the head of his wilting cock, tasting him for the first time. With one finger I sweep up the liquid deposit from his abdomen then lick the finger clean. I slide myself up his body and, clasping my fingers in his hair, I kiss him, letting his come flow from my mouth into his. He struggles, but I do not release him until I feel him swallow, then I pull away until I am standing before him.

He looks a different man now. His hair has lost the slick, groomed appearance and is now nicely tousled, like he's been working the land. His tanned body does nothing to distract from that image and the layer of sweat that is making his skin gleam and reflecting the overhead lighting adds to the illusion. He'd look perfectly natural rising up from the hay in a smelly old barn, a million miles away from his usual "Mr Perfect" pose. I like him better this way, it's more honest.

I cannot help but laugh at the confusion of expressions playing on his face, he is not used to yielding to another, his ego struggles to resist, but the rest of his being is yearning to continue, no matter how humiliating it becomes. I dip my finger into his glass and suck off the drops of wine I collect. "Maybe you need something sweeter to taste," I suggest and my finger is dipped again but this time I back against the desk and the drips of wine are smeared between my legs.

He climbs from the chair and falls to his knees before me. Ego has lost. He is ready to worship and I tilt my pelvis towards him and part my legs to accept his supplication. His breath reaches me first, sending a shiver of anticipation through me, making my clit stand even prouder, a pearl of desire ready to accept its dues. "Lick me!" I order and his tongue does as I bid.

He is so tentative at first, barely touching, I feel no pressure just a sensation of warmth and moisture. It feels so good, but it is not enough, my body demands more and I cannot hold back the throaty groan that reveals my need. I thrust forward and draw him closer to me by wrapping my thighs over his shoulders. "Harder!" I demand. Even now his tongue is soft and gentle, caressing and exploring. He laps against my clit like waves breaking on the shore, every so often sweeping down and exploring the hollow between my lips collecting the juices as they invite him to penetrate me. His fingers inch towards my opening but I clench my pelvic floor and deny him entry. Instead I tell him to use his hands to hold the labia open and expose even more of my clit so I can savour every second of the magic his tongue is working.

He does as I command and his tongue becomes more urgent, pressing hard against my clit, lapping faster and harder, the intensity is pure ecstasy and I tell him to keep going. The feeling builds ever more strongly and I know that the blissful release is close, but I need even more. I twist my fingers in his hair and pull him even closer, riding on the waves of sensation now pulsing through my body. "Bite it!" I cry and he presses my clit against his teeth with his tongue making the sensation sharper and impossible to resist. "I said bite it!" I command and for a second my grip in his hair is painfully tight, until he is squeezing my eager clit between his teeth and I relax my hold. Now when his tongue brushes over me every sensation is magnified and the peak is attained.

My legs tremble and I collapse against the table as my cunt begins to clench as spasm after spasm of delicious orgasm explodes through me. My grasp on his hair does not totally relax and he is forced to continue his ministrations until I am completely sated and push him away.

He sinks back to the floor and looks at me. His eyes are heavy with desire and his cock is hard again and straining to respond to my body's invitation. "Please," he asks and I know that all he is aware of is how much he wants me. He is mine and he knows he will never be my master.

My body is still twitching and pulsing from the sensations he has caused and I am tempted. It would feel so good to ride him, and even after that magnificent orgasm part of me yearns to be filled with his hard male strength, to share the surrender. But today is a not a day for weakness, and right now his need for me is handing me all the power and mastery he has ever tried to wield. He is my slave and I am the Mistress he desires with every fibre of his being.

"Don't be stupid" I say. "I would never sleep with the boss," and collecting my clothes I leave him naked on the floor, too proud to come after me and too broken to think of anything else. Alpha male put firmly in his place.

Best of all, whether this night is repeated many times or never talked of again, when he swaggers past my desk in future we will both know that, whatever impression he gives to the rest of the office, his true place is right there grovelling naked at my feet.

Man-Stalker
by Landon Dixon

Detective Ovitz threw the picture down on the table in disgust. "C'mon, Dooley!" he bellowed. "We know it's her, you know it's her – so identify her already! You wanna take the rap all by yourself?"

Calvin Dooley adjusted his glasses with trembling hands, staring at the mugshot of the pretty young woman with the big brown eyes and long brown hair – the full, sensuous mouth smiling confidently into the police camera. He *thought* she looked familiar … but he just couldn't be sure.

"She had you steal five million dollars from the bank, Calvin," Detective Morgan tried, much more gently than his partner. "Then stole it from you. We know that. She's done it to three other stoog– … men that we know of; important men in important positions of trust like yours – seduced them, suckered them into stealing, and then walked off with the loot. But not one's been able to positively …"

Calvin's mind tuned out the detective's plea, catching and focusing on that one word he'd said – 'walked'. He smiled dreamily up into the harsh light of the interrogation room, his thoughts drifting back to the day that Eva La Flora had first walked into his life …

He'd been working under his model train set-up in the

garage, repairing a leg on the platform, when a sultry voice had suddenly said, "Excuse me, I seem to be lost."

He'd crawled out on his hands and knees from under the platform and straight into the most perfectly-formed, erotically-shaped set of female lower limbs he'd ever laid eyes on. Delicately slender and taut, yet deliciously curved in all the right places, gleaming bare and smooth and golden in the slanting summer sun; size 8 feet poised and presented in high-heeled sandals that artfully displayed every slim, succulent, gold-tipped toe, the twin graceful, breathtaking arches and the finely-constructed, finger-enwrapping ankles. A silver ring shone on the middle toe of the right foot, a silver anklet twinkling on the left leg.

Calvin's star-struck eyes travelled up, way up the beautiful skyscraper legs, his breath coming shorter and his cock getting harder as his eyes climbed ever higher. For his was a raging leg fetish that had sprung up way back in junior high – when he'd first glimpsed the lean, tanned gams of his new gym teacher, Ms Parisienne, in her tiny, little white short-shorts – and had spread like a wildfire obsession to encompass his entire adult life. Two failed marriages and a basement full of magazines, books, and DVDs, women's stockings, pantyhose, and shoes, were testimony to his lifetime of leg worship.

"Lost?" he gulped, transfixed by the poured-gold limbs.

And Eva La Flora, looking down from her sandaled pedestals at the awestruck bank executive on the ground at her feet, knew she had her man.

He invited her inside his house, ostensibly to consult a city map for the 'Limbledon Drive' she was searching for, though they were both pretty sure no such street existed in the small Midwestern city. She perched on the edge of a brown leather wingback chair in Calvin's living room, in her pale green shorts and white halter top, long, caramel-coated legs crossed and spilling out all over the floor, dazzling Calvin still more.

He jumped around pouring lemonade into a glass, piling cookies onto a platter. Only when he ran to Eva with the shaking tray and sweating glass, she 'accidentally' kicked out her dangling foot and tripped him. The lemonade and cookies went flying. And were forgotten. Because Eva had her man exactly where she wanted him now, exactly where he wanted to be – on the floor at her feet in the privacy of his own home.

He gaped at her recrossed limbs from two feet away. She wagged her right leg slightly, her right foot picking up the rhythm. Calvin inhaled the sweet fanned perfume, his ears full of the silky rustle of leg flesh, his eyes following the bobbing toe ring like a puppy follows its master. Sweat streamed down his face and his glasses fogged up, the room gone stifling, the air breathless, as he ate up the woman's gold-painted toes and golden limbs, patiently and impatiently waiting.

Eva finally sighed, and uncrossed her legs in a velvet symphony. Her right foot touched down on the hardwood floor in front of the fallen man. "You can touch," she allowed.

Calvin's heart leapt, along with his hands. He brushed her arch with his quivering fingertips, tracing the sculpted roundness, the smooth-as-satin skin. Then he quickly lost control and recklessly grabbed onto the sensually-structured feminine appendage and smothered it with kisses, desperate to taste the spiced-leather heated richness of Eva's foot.

She jerked it away. "Behave yourself! You'll do as I say, and take what I give you."

He dropped his head and hands, and nodded.

Leg men were fanatics, Eva well-knew, willing, anxious to bend to the whims of a woman's well-turned lower limbs. And she'd done her research well, for Calvin was truly a leg man starving for stem, famished for feet. A leg-crazy sucker she now had in the instep of her foot.

She stayed for dinner, for the weekend, moved in with Calvin, bringing nothing more with her than a spectacular set of gams. Which to Calvin was everything. And gradually she let him touch her bare feet again, stroke and caress and pet them, baby them with oils and lotions, groom them with emery board and toenail polish.

And as the heated days and nights passed, Eva allowed Calvin's covetous hands to roam higher – up and around her ankles, his fingers tightening on the taut tendons at the back of the slim joints; up and down her impossibly long shins; behind onto the dainty, pliable masses of her calves, the feel of the muscles clenching and bunching in the palms of his hands sending him sailing; up along to the baby-soft, vulnerable backs of her knees, his fingertips swirling all over the sensitive skin. Until finally, finally his hands were allowed to wander all the way up and into the meaty, golden flesh of her thighs, his fingers digging into the supple muscles, revelling in the warm expanse of velvety skin.

It was two weeks into their relationship, when Calvin was carefully pampering Eva's feet before putting them to bed, that she proposed he supplement his income, and her legs, with some extra cash from the bank.

"You mean st-steal it?" he gasped, gripping the soft, curved soles of her feet.

She looked down at him on the floor from over her knees. "'Embezzle', I believe, is the correct term." Her glossy lips parted in a smile, the first Calvin had ever received from her. "You work so hard at the bank and yet they pay you so little. It's not fair."

"Well, it *is* a pretty small bank, even by this state's standards," Calvin reflected. Before her idea hit home again. "But-but I've been with Mr Laudermilk and the bank for twelve years …" he began to protest.

Until Eva lifted her right foot out of his hands and up to his mouth. She pressed her big toe against his lips, silencing him, reminding him what it was really all about.

He thrilled at the touch of her smooth, bulbed foot-digit against his lips. He shot his hands up and grabbed onto her foot, inhaling her edible toe and nursing on it like a child its thumb. He sucked and sucked on her big toe, as she watched him, foot arching in his hands, sole crinkling delightfully.

"You're in charge of business loans, aren't you?" Eva purred, saucily curling her toes as Calvin disgorged her biggest and furiously squirmed his tongue in between the others, up and down the line.

"Y-yes," he gulped, concentrating on sucking, tugging on her plump-topped toes, one at a time, popping them in and out of his mouth in a frenzy. He scoured the elegantly rounded ball of her foot with his tongue as he sucked.

"Well … you could set up some dummy companies, write up the paperwork, approve the loans, and then funnel the money into outside bank accounts that you controlled, couldn't you?"

"I could," he rasped. He swallowed up all of her glistening, wiggling toes, and half of her foot, willing to agree to anything so long as she allowed him to devour her feet.

"You will," Eva informed him, pulling her ped away. "So you can keep my legs and feet in the manner to which they're accustomed."

"I will! I will!" Calvin wailed, grabbing onto her ankle and urgently lapping at her sole. He dragged his tongue from little balled heel to exuberant toe-tips in long, sloppy licks, thrilling at the erotic contours his tongue painted, the amazing softness and smoothness of her pale, unpuckered foot-bottom.

She kicked him in the chin, and he staggered back on his

knees. He dropped his hands down to his sides, his head down to his chest. And watched forlornly as Eva strutted away from him on her tip-toes, calves pumping and soles flashing.

He put her plan into action the very next day at the bank, defrauding his employer just as she'd outlined. As a trusted VP with signing authority – his portfolio of loans only subject to monthly review by the bank president, Mr Laudermilk – it was remarkably easy.

He used some of the transferred and then quickly withdrawn funds to shower Eva's legs with gifts: the finest imported silk and nylon-crafted stockings, of all colours and patterns, adorned with all manner of ribbons and bows; obscenely high heeled designer shoes and boots of outrageous beauty and cost, impossibly tall and sharp stilettos and phone book-thick platforms that raised the woman's luscious legs and feet to new heights in the air, above him; and expensive, hand-tooled ankle and toe jewellery of all kinds brought back from the big city. The rest of the money he kept in his basement safe, at Eva's suggestion again. Cash on hand to keep her lower limbs in luxury well into the future, Calvin happily thought.

And it was on the night that he proposed marriage – four weeks into their relationship – that she finally gave him the greatest gift any leggy lady can bestow on her dedicated footman: complete and utter foot fulfilment.

Calvin crawled across the living room floor towards her, a fifty-thousand-dollar five-carat diamond ring in a platinum setting clenched between his teeth. Eva was sitting in her chair studying travel brochures, legs sheathed in brilliant, snow-white stockings, feet shod in red leather five-inch stilettos.

He crawled up to her feet on the floor, then shyly looked up at her, expectation and anxiety written all over his face and in his eyes. She regarded him with her usual disdain, until she spotted the precious gem in his mouth. Her brown eyes flared, then subsided. She coolly nodded assent, and Calvin almost swallowed the ring in his excitement and joy.

He jumped to his knees and took hold of her left foot, expertly unwinding the straps on the sexy shoe and sliding it off her silken ped, heel to toe. The shoe dropped to the floor. "Your st-stocking will have to come off," he slobbered through gritted teeth, and the ring.

She sighed, set down the brochures, and unhooked the lacy vanilla stocking top from the crimson-bowed white garter straps that lay just under her slash of a scarlet leather skirt. The trimmed black fur of her pussy was on display as she executed the erotic manoeuvre, but Calvin hardly noticed. His unblinking eyes were on the stocking, as she slowly slid it down her limb, revealing more and more smooth, golden skin that shone in the light from the tableside lamp.

She pulled the stocking away from the tip of her ped, fully baring her leg, wriggling her delectable piggies like a wave goodbye to the leg dressing as she lifted it away. Calvin spat the ring into one hand and grasped her sole with the other. He slipped the ring onto her wedding toe – a perfect fit, as they both knew it would be.

Eva smiled, staring at the big diamond on her foot. She waggled her long-stemmed toes, the stone sparkling with even more intensity than her gold toenail polish. Then she remembered the gleefully grinning man in front of her, and she slipped the empty stocking over his head, intoxicating Calvin with the residual scent and heat of her leg and foot.

She rolled the sister stocking off her other leg, putting on a show for the panting stocking-head. He tried to grab onto her nude peds, but she brushed his sweaty paws away with her feet and said, "Pull your pants down."

He fumbled his belt buckle and fly open and jammed his Dockers down. "Your shorts," she said. And he shoved them down, his cock bounding up hard and yearning as he stood on his knees before her.

Eva leaned back in her chair and extended her luxuriant legs, unfolding them like the sensuous instruments of torture and pleasure they were. She pointed her perfect toes and slowly and steadily brought the balls of her feet together, on either side of Calvin's straining erection. He jumped, moaned, the exquisite, superheated feel of her peds on his cock bringing a tear of pre-come shooting up to his slit, real tears springing into his adoring, bespectacled eyes and clotting the mesh of Eva's stocking.

He could hardly believe it was finally happening – his cock was actually between her beautiful feet, her glorious, jewelled toes caressing his vein-popped shaft. His whole body vibrated, his being flooding with a heavy, heady, tingling heat.

"You've been fairly good to me," Eva allowed. Her toes dipped down to touch his balls, then slid back up his shaft, stroking his raging cock with her feet.

He swallowed his Adam's apple, fists clenched and body full-out shaking, the stocking on his head bellowing in front of his mouth; desperately willing himself to hold off desecrating her heavenly feet with his unholy semen, to revel in the soul-shattering sensation of her wicked peds caressing his undeserving cock for as long as possible.

"And you're going to be even better to me," Eva added. Before unfooting his cock, telling him to stand up and strip naked.

When Calvin had done as she'd ordered, Eva rose to her feet and tied the man's hands behind his back with the second stocking. Then she led him by the prick into her bedroom, his eyes glued to the ballerina movements of her legs every step of the way. She towed him to the foot of the bed, pushed him down onto his back. And then, as his eyes popped like flashbulbs, she climbed onto the bed and on top of him, proceeding to literally walk all over him.

She was light as a feather, strolling up his undulating stomach and onto his heaving chest. Her toes clenched his hardened nipples, and he fought for breath through his stocking top. She towered over him high as any woman can go on a grateful man, her golden legs gleaming skyscrapers that he could never hope to fully scale, or explore, but would commit a lifetime to trying. She stood on his chest and lifted her left ped and dipped her toes down onto his face. His stockinged mouth futilely tried to swallow the teasing foot-digits and suck on them, the diamond ring winking derisively at him.

And after walking all over him, Eva had Calvin squirm higher up on the bed. Then she dropped down between his trembling legs and leaned back and extended her honey-coated limbs again. Her left foot landed soft and silky as an angel's wing on his jumping cock on his stomach, the toes of her right foot nuzzling his balls.

Calvin groaned sweet agony, arching his body off the bed to meet her tantalizing feet, as she feathered his pulsating shaft with the toes of her one foot, juggled his tightened sac with the toes of the other. And when she heeled the base of his cock and shot his shaft upright, he just couldn't take it anymore, his dreams coming true in a geyser of semen.

"Oh, Jesus, God!" he cried, his cock exploding under Eva's feet. Sperm boiled out of his pressed-down sac and jetted out of his toe-tickled cap, splashing down onto his chest and stomach in great, gooey ropes.

He lay back on the bed gasping for air, his head swimming and body smouldering, balls empty like never before. But over his strangled breathing, he heard Eva's delicate peds touch down on the floor and pad away, lovely legs swishing together. He flung his head to the side only in time to catch one final glimpse of her superbly-shaped stems and hourglass soles, as they walked out of the room and out of his life ...

The two detectives glared at the stupidly-grinning sap in the hot seat, shaking their heads in frustration.

Then the door to the interrogation room popped open, and Officer Beeker stuck his head inside. "How's it going?" he asked.

"Lousy," Detective Ovitz growled. "Just like with the others. What'd you want, anyway, Beeker?"

"Well, I know I'm new and all," the patrolman said, slipping into the room. "But I've been kind of studying the case, and, uh, the woman involved, and I think I've got something that might help." He placed a photograph down on the table in front of Calvin. And the man's eyes lit up and he leapt out of his chair, pointing at the picture. "That's her! That's her!" he screamed.

Ovitz and Beeker had to hold Calvin down, as Detective Morgan rushed to the door and yelled for a stenographer. Then they all looked at the new mugshot of Eva La Flora – from the waist down this time, her long, lithe, golden legs glowing gorgeous even in the harsh light of the police station booking room.

"Good work," Ovitz grunted at the rookie cop.

Beeker grinned, like Calvin, staring at the picture.

His Lordship's New Mistress
by Virginia Beech

Dusk was falling and the lamplighters were already out tending to the gaslamps when Freya von Hohenfels alighted from the Hansom cab at Camberley House, 63 Grosvenor Square in Mayfair. The 25-year-old Prussian was tired after her two-day journey from Berlin and looking forward to taking up her appointment as Housekeeper at the residence of Hubert Wadsworth, the bachelor Earl of Camberley.

She found herself before the portal of an extravagantly styled house that reflected the self-importance of its occupant who was making a fortune importing guano birdshit from the South Atlantic to satisfy the demands of Victorian horticulturalists for exotic fertiliser in their exotic conservatories.

The front door was opened by a tall, striking, auburn-haired butlerine dressed in a sensuously severe uniform of 'Duchess Satin' that contoured her well-rounded shape.

Freya entered an opulent world far removed from her Prussian upbringing. The majestic hallway was illuminated by a glittering chandelier that lit up the painted ceiling of cavorting nymphs and the life-size painting of harem girls by Lord Leighton which hung in gold-leafed splendour over a marble fireplace. A gleaming floor led to a sweeping stairway, its intricate wrought-iron banisters ending in ornate pedestals supporting Italianate marble statuary.

The butlerine took Freya's cloak and bonnet, handing them to a bewigged footman.

"James will take your things to your room."

She looked appreciatively at the well-endowed, young Prussian. "Welcome to our Household! I am Davison, the butlerine. Please call me Cordelia. I do hope we'll be friends." She smiled. "Rumours of your caning expertise precede you. If his Lordship has his way, there will be sore bottoms below stairs!"

She gave a provocative wiggle of her butt, so obligingly outlined by her uniform. "I hope you won't be caning my own rump," she laughed, "but you are welcome to discipline the stable lads if the Earl will let you near them. Their randy buttocks could do with a stinging Prussian kiss. From what I gather, his Lordship has more than..."

The Earl's stable activities were left unsaid, as she led the way across the hall to his study.

"His Lordship will see you immediately. Afterwards I'll show you your room."

She lowered her voice. "Be warned! He's a swine and if he can sow discord between the servants, he will. We only put up with his whims because he pays well."

Cordelia cordially squeezed Freya's hand, knocked discreetly, and ushered her in.

"The new Housekeeper has arrived, my Lord."

The interview that Friday evening with Hubert Wadsworth, Earl of Camberley, was painfully memorable.

Seated at his ornate desk, the 43-year-old Master of the House motioned Freya forward. She curtseyed and drew from her reticule the letter of introduction from Frau Brenner, Principal of the Berlin Academy.

He broke the seal and read the letter. "Have you experience of the cane?"

Such intimacy caught Freya off guard. "Frau Brenner

sometimes caned us for slovenly academic work."

"Did she use something like this?" The Earl brought out a rattan from behind the desk and laid it on the tooled-leather surface. Thanks to his correspondence with Frau Brenner over Freya's suitability, the Earl was well aware of her background. Frau Brenner had written of the occasions she had bared her bottom for a public caning at Assembly. The rattan would bring painful memories.

"I require a Housekeeper who knows what a well-padded posterior is for!" He sniggered. "Servants need frequent caning and Frau Irma, whose place you are taking, now she has retired, never spared the rod."

The Earl's buttocks tingled at the pleasant memory of Irma's personal ministrations; when she spanked him over her knee, strapped his bared bottom in her bedroom, or more recently, in secret caning sessions behind the locked door of his study.

"Your Principal is most fulsome about your disciplinary dominance."

"Frau Brenner taught me well, my Lord."

Freya thought of the plump Prussian posteriors she had bared, when, as Head Girl, she inflicted the canings she had herself once endured. She remembered also Frau Brenner's secret Sapphic rituals in her boudoir afterwards.

"You will hand me a list of servant transgressions every Friday morning before parading the miscreants for punishment in my study. The stables at the back in Adams Row are not your responsibility. *I* deal with discipline there."

"I understand you perfectly, my Lord," Freya replied, remembering Cordelia's remark in the hallway. "I am an adept caner. I take pleasure and pride in Discipline."

Lord Camberley smiled. "Excellent! You Prussians bring such robust finesse to punishment procedures. I look forward to witnessing your expertise."

He smirked, took a pinch of Kendal Brown snuff, snorted and sneezed.

"Indeed, you shall commence your duties right now. Bare Davison's bottom and cane her before me! The arrogant bitch thinks she runs this place."

A startled butlerine looked at Camberley's smug face.

"Put her over the armchair and whip some humility into her! My endorsement of you as Housekeeper, together with Davison's continued employment rests solely upon your ability to suitably humiliate her with a sound thrashing. I venture to opine that you will find her posterior perfectly proportioned for punishment."

"No! You wouldn't dare!" Cordelia gasped in disbelief.

"I've had enough of your tittle-tattle about my stable activities, Davison. If you wish to remain in service here, you will give me the infinite pleasure of seeing your bottom caned."

Freya was in an impossible position. Cordelia's refusal to submit would cost them both their places. She knew that she must assert her new authority immediately to save their positions. She fixed the butlerine with a piercing look.

"Bend over that armchair! Now!"

Cordelia hesitated, then complied. Her moment of defiance had passed. Freya had control. Taking a black kidskin glove from her reticule, she eased it onto her caning hand, picked up the rattan to inspect it with an experienced eye and moved to the butlerine's side.

"We must humour the *Schwein*," she whispered, "but we'll make him pay. He'll regret this day! I'll take you in my arms tonight, *Liebling* and we'll forget this in the heat of our passion."

She flipped Cordelia's skirt over her back and eased down her knickers to bare a plump bottom. "I'll cane you with love," she whispered, caressing the bared curves. "You'll enjoy my love caning. But we must make it look as if I'm hurting you. Scream and cry, while you think of us together tonight when I kiss each lovestripe on your beautiful *Arsch*."

Cordelia wiggled her butt to show acceptance.

"Open your legs and stretch those knickers between your knees."

Freya turned to the Earl. "I require full view of a miscreant's *Arsch* in order to cane her properly. You can see your butlerine has a classic "chubby" bottom. It's ideal for caning and presents a visually pleasing picture, *nicht war*?"

She patted Cordelia's upturned spheres, receiving another wiggle from her now willing partner in deception.

Despite his preference for a groom's bared buttocks with virile upstanding cock and balls attached, Camberley was aroused. Freya noted a nascent bulge in his trousers. She brushed her hand against its throbbing warmth and their eyes met in mutual understanding. Housekeeper and butlerine would be secure at Camberley House after this.

"I now inspect a miscreant for any wetness indicating wanton arousal. Sluttish lasciviousness warrants additional punishment strokes applied with extra vigour."

The feel of Freya's finger probing her pussy for moist arousal produced just that effect on Cordelia, as she thought of Freya's promised night of love.

"Get on with it before I flood with desire for you in front of that swine," Cordelia hissed. "And do be kind to my bottom!"

Freya gave her clitoris a reassuring tweak with her probing fingers before taking up her caning stance.

"Take Punishment Posture!"

Cordelia arched her back obediently, presenting her rounded charms to the Earl's leering gaze.

"See where bottom curves into thigh? That's the most tender part. We call it the 'sweet spot'."

Freya rubbed the cane along the imaginary line she had described, eliciting a theatrical whimper of apprehension and anticipatory quiver of desire from her fellow conspirator.

"You will register each stroke. Call out its number and thank me. *Verstanden*?"

A muffled "Yes, Miss Hohenfels," came from the armchair.

Freya brought her arm slowly back and swung.

Crack!

The cut seared across the twin globes, landing unerringly on the soft 'sweet spot' to leave an instant crimson mark.

"Aaah! One! Thank you, Miss Hohenfels!"

"I pause between each stroke," Freya commented, running her hand gently over the red weal. "Chubby cheeks quiver and wobble most endearingly at each cut and successful punishment requires time and tension for maximum impact."

Five more strokes followed. Freya paused after each stroke and tenderly caressed Cordelia's cheeks; a secret love bonding between Domina and Submissive. The aroused Earl was unaware of such subtlety. Hand in pocket, he was covertly stroking his heated cock.

Freya shifted her position for the last stroke. "I call this final stroke 'The Gate' . I place it diagonally across the others to join them together like a crossbar."

Crack!

The stroke seared across the five parallel cuts, uniting them in the promised pattern; an unexpectedly warm memento of Freya's arrival in Cordelia's life and heart.

"Six!" Cordelia sobbed theatrically. Freya's lovecaning had unleashed deep and hitherto dormant emotions in her bosom, bringing tears to her eyes. Her final "Thank you, Miss Hohenfels!" was whispered with love.

Freya contemplated the parallel lines of red she had

etched across Cordelia's rounded spheres with the professional pride of an experienced dominatrix. By the morrow they would be a deeper shade of purple; a pleasing reminder of what she hoped would be the first of many lovecanings for Cordelia.

"Adjust your clothing!" she ordered quickly, before Camberley could sully Cordelia's exposure with his hand. But his voyeuristic lust was sated. He had stroked himself to orgasm in his trousers. A damp stain at his crotch bore sticky witness to his covert handplay.

Freya smiled knowingly and moved closer to him.

"Punishment is completed, my Lord. To your satisfaction, I see!"

She squeezed the subsiding bulge in his trousers. A sterner note crept into her voice.

"I punish naughty boys who masturbate. Be here at 10 o'clock sharp, tomorrow morning!" She slapped the cane against her skirted calf, to emphasise just what punishment this naughty boy should expect from a Prussian Dominatrix.

A dreamy look came over Hubert's face. Memories of Irma's weekly discipline ritual flooded back. Rubbing himself to orgasm over Irma's knee as she spanked his bared bottom he would ejaculate over her. She would make him kneel to lick his cum off her thighs and knickers. Sucking at the wet fabric, he would inhale her heady fragrance through the silk. Happy days are here again! He nodded in anticipation.

"Did my predecessor dress you up for punishment?" It was an intuitively leading question.

"Yes, Fräulein Hohenfels."

Bullseye! The Earl was a closet transvestite submissive!

"Dress appropriately for Mistress then!"

Taking Cordelia protectively by the arm, the new Housekeeper swept from the study.

She would be Mistress of Camberley House on the

morrow.

Upstairs in her room, Freya took Cordelia to her bosom.

"My poor *Liebling*! The Master is a *Schwein* and we shall repay him for humiliating you. I shall be Mistress of this house with you at my side before that *Scheissloch* sits down to dinner tomorrow. He will lick our boots! And now let me see that pretty *Arsch* of yours."

The butlerine gazed adoringly into Freya's Nordic blue eyes.

"Do not reproach yourself! We had to do it. And I felt safe in your power because every sweet stroke told me you desire me. While I was bent over I imagined you stripping me naked and taking me. I wanted to submit willingly, totally and unconditionally to you there and then. But not with that pervert looking on."

Freya's heart skipped at Cordelia's words. She slid her hands sensuously down over the ample breasts and luscious curves of her hips.

"Leave me for half an hour, *Liebling,* while I wash and prepare for our exciting night of love."

When Cordelia returned, she had changed into a softly flowing *décolleté* gown of russet silk. She had wantonly let her hair down. A tumult of auburn tresses cascaded over her shoulders and breasts in wild abandon.

Their exploratory kiss began as the softest brush of lips. It was the spark that fired the tinder of Cordelia's latent lust; a lascivious flame of desire heightened by the glowing warmth of her caned bottom cheeks.

Cordelia kicked the door shut.

Freya's serpentine tongue sought entry between Cordelia's full lips. They parted obediently and then, as passion flamed, with abandon, to take Freya's thrusting tongue hungrily. Cordelia sucked voraciously, pressing her breasts and belly hard against her Nordic conqueror.

"Tonguefuck me," she panted. "Storm my defences, you beautiful, thrilling, desirable, dominating Junker fucker! Show no mercy!"

Freya backed Cordelia toward her bed, easing her diaphanous gown off her shoulders as she went.

"Your dress is ravishing, *Liebling*. But it's time to remove it."

Cordelia began to tug at the restraining sash.

"N*ein! Liebling! I* plunder! *You* submit!"

She ripped Cordelia's gown from breast to belly, tearing it from her body to reveal her black sateen corset. It perfectly moulded the curvaceous contours of her body; crushed diamonds dipped in liquid jet. Thrusting up the full glory of her breasts, it accentuated the slimness of her waist before expanding in voluptuously smooth curves to frame her satin-knickered bottom.

For the second time that day Freya eased those knickers down to reveal a silky fleece of pussy curls. They bushed out, erotically framed by the corset and its taut suspender straps holding her stockings to her thighs.

She ran her hands over Cordelia's corseted curves, delving to release and display her imprisoned breasts in their full, rounded beauty. Cordelia posed provocatively, cupping them, enticing her Domina to suckle and nibble at the ripe globes.

"Disrobe me!"

Cordelia tore obediently at Freya's dress, baring her upright breasts with their powder pink aureoles and prominent nipples. She bent and flicked one with her tongue and then sucked it to hardened arousal. Her hands strayed south to pull silk knickers down. Freya kicked them off and stood proudly back.

Cordelia's eyes widened in startled surprise. Strapped to Freya's hips was a black leather dildo, its virile length now unleashed from its silken confines and rampantly erect;

swaying... beckoning.

"Meet 'Thor's Hammer' ! Suck!"

Cordelia knelt reverently to take the leather tool between her lips. Freya grasped her head brusquely and thrust, sliding the cuntcock deep into her mouth, jerking Cordelia's head back and forth to her hard thrusts, enjoying her gurgled sucking and the massaging vibrations transmitted to the alter-dildo nestling within her vagina's tight grip.

Cordelia's hand strayed to her pussy, sought her clitoris and began to finger herself to wet excitement for Freya's impending shafting.

Freya withdrew her cuntcock, wet and glistening from its facefucking, picked Cordelia up and threw her down onto the bed.

She covered her with her body. "First I ride you! Then I tonguefuck you!"

Rubbing the tip of her cuntcock against Cordelia's now dripping cunt and throbbing clit, Freya raised her buttocks and thrust 'Thor's Hammer' deep into her yielding belly.

The pinioned girl gasped at the thrusting shaft's girth. "Oh, darling! Oh, wonderful darling! Fuck me! Fuck me! Possess me!"

She bucked to meet Freya's thrusting rhythm. "Yes! Darling! You Goddess studfucker! Deeper! Take me! Hammer me!"

A passionate kiss reduced her to muffled ecstatic incoherence.

Freya's nostrils flared with passion. She quickened her thrusting rhythm as the juices of her coming orgasm began to flow. Gripping the reddened plumpness of Cordelia's bottom cheeks, she split them apart to thrust her finger deep, feeling the pounding of her cuntcock through the vaginal wall.

"Aah uh! Aah uh! Aah uh!"

Cordelia's breath came in rasping pants; a staccato beat

to that thrusting hammer. Her orgasm rose, welling up inside her belly; a burning fire that glowed and fizzed around her blood-engorged clitoris, spreading up through her tingling body.

"I'm coming! Oh! Goddess! I'm coming! Fuck me! Fuck me! Aaaaaah!"

Exhortations turned to gurgled delirium as Cordelia's orgasm took hold, flared and exploded within her plundered body, pulsating through her in sweet waves of joy.

The flood brought Freya to her own passionate climax. She stiffened, hammering a final orgasmic thrust into the quivering butlerine before collapsing in sweating ecstasy upon her breasts as the shock waves raced through her.

Her defences stormed, Cordelia lay in contented surrender beneath her lover, luxuriating in the delicious feel of the black leather monster filling her cunt.

"Welcome to Camberley House, my magnificent Valkyrie! Plunder and pillage my pussy every starry night! Give no quarter!"

Freya smiled triumphantly and kissed the hot face beneath her. She licked the beads of sweat glistening on Cordelia's breasts.

"Let me whisper a secret in your ear. Tomorrow, I spank Hubert Wadsworth. He was Frau Irma's secret transvestite submissive. She spanked him regularly."

Cordelia's eyes widened in surprise. "So that's why they were closeted every Saturday morning in his locked study!"

Freya nibbled absentmindedly at a large nipple.

"Tomorrow, that *Scheissloch* will worship me after I impose my will as his new Mistress. Our revenge will be sweeter than your cum juices, my *Liebling*!"

She withdrew her slick and glistening cuntcock slowly from the moist grip of Cordelia's pussy and picked up her knickers.

"Clean my dildo on these."

A mystified Cordelia dried its glistening shaft on them.

Freya put the impregnated silk to her nose, savouring the aroma of their lovejuices.

"Perfect! They'll be handy when I spank that noble *Arsch* in the morning," she confided enigmatically.

"Unstrap me now, my *Liebling*, and run us a bath while I tell you what I have in mind for him tomorrow... and every Saturday morning thereafter."

Attired in spurred boots and tight-waisted black riding habit that accentuated her goddess-like figure, Freya walked authoritatively into the Earl's study the following morning.

She closed the door and turned the key. He was seated behind his desk, waiting expectantly.

Freya strode firmly across the room. "Little boys rise and say, 'Good Morning, Mistress!' when I enter. My predecessor appears to have let discipline slip. I won't have that."

She slapped her riding quirt against her booted calf. "Come out from behind that desk at once!"

"Yes, Mistress! Good Morning, Mistress!"

He had dressed in white satin and lace shirt, black velveteen knickerbockers, matching hose and silver-buckled pumps; a throwback to Irma's punishment ritual.

"First you shall learn about the proper use of your right hand. Hold it out, palm upward!"

Freya whipped her quirt down sharply.

Thwack!

"Your right hand is for holding your fork at table..."

Thwack!

"For writing with your pen..."

Thwack!

"For doffing your cap to Mistress..."

Thwack!

"It is NOT..."

Thwack!

"For masturbating! You dirty little boy!"

Tears of pain filled Hubert's eyes as his hand reddened under Mistress's stinging quirt.

"When did Irma last put you over her knee, Hubert?"

"The night before she left, Mistress."

"And for what naughtiness, Hubert?"

"For looking up her skirt, Mistress."

"And what did she do, Hubert?"

"She made me drop my drawers. Then she put me over her knee and hand-spanked me."

"Was that all, Hubert?"

"No, Mistress! Then she strapped me for being dirty."

"What dirtiness, Hubert?"

"I came on her knickers when she spanked me, Mistress."

"Beastly boy! From that bulge in your breeches, Mistress can see you are still mired in moral turpitude. Mistress shall spank you for your disgusting thoughts, Hubert!"

Craven desire illuminated Hubert's face. Now was the moment for Dominatrix to impose total dominance and accept total submission.

"I am your Mistress! You shall appear every Saturday morning properly dressed for punishment. Mistress shall spank you as you confess all. Is that clear?"

Hubert's look turned to unconcealed adoration. "Yes, Mistress! I am very naughty. I deserve your spanking."

"Drop your breeches!"

Hubert unbuttoned his knickerbockers and stepped out of them. He was wearing voluminous pink silk knickers laced at the knee. The semi-transparent material barely concealed his erection throbbing in anticipation of the promised spanking from this goddess-like Nordic Dominatrix.

"Why are you wearing lady's knickers, Hubert?"

"They are Frau Irma's, Mistress. She made me wear

them to cure me of my dirty habits. But it didn't. I always came when she spanked me."

Freya rasped a long fingernail over his tent-pole erection. "Mistress must prescribe stronger medicine for Hubert. Perhaps these will cure you."

She withdrew her aromatically soiled silk knickers from her bodice.

"Put these on. You will wear them every Saturday for your spanking."

He held their damp fragrance to his face, greedily inhaling their cumjuice perfume before dropping Irma's old bloomers, to pull their delicate femininity over his rampant cock.

Sitting down, Freya hitched up her skirt and motioned for Hubert to bend over her lap. He positioned himself readily, throbbing cock hard against her welcoming thigh.

Freya caressed his butt, kneading and playing 'pinch bottom' through the tautly stretched silk.

"You are a dirty little boy, Hubert. Your naughty Winkie is rubbing against Mistress's knee. Mr Smack must visit Miss Bottom!"

Exposing Hubert's cheeks, she began to spank each bouncy sphere in turn, spreading a heated blush to the quivering globes squirming on her lap.

Hubert's first grunts turned to moans of pleasure at Freya's stinging hand. She felt a pre-cum wetness on her knee as he wriggled and ground in frenzied friction against sensual softness of her thighs.

Suddenly the blows ceased.

A warm hand explored between the cleft of Hubert's glowing cheeks and glided delicately between his legs.

"Are we still harbouring filthy thoughts, Hubert!"

Fingers fondled his warm jewels.

"Dirty boy! Still consumed with lust!"

He squirmed in panting thrill as fingers explored up his

pulsating shaft; a soft caress gently easing its tight foreskin to and fro over the blood-engorged glans, urging it to ecstatic release.

"Disgusting child! Mistress must exorcise these lewd desires!"

The hand gripped his shaft more firmly, moving sensuously up and down its pulsating heat, pumping it urgently now. Hubert's sap rose uncontrollably to the quickening rhythm of Mistress's magic. He came in quivering explosive ecstasy, jerking hot streams of creamy spend into her hand.

"Aaah! Mistress! Spank me! Spank naughty Hubert!"

He squirted a final spasm of buttermilk and lay spent across Mistress's lap, his cum oozing between her fingers onto her knickered thigh.

"Filthy child! You have messed on Mistress's knickers! How dare you, Hubert!"

She gave his crimson cheeks a flurry of hard slaps before pushing him off her knee.

"Kneel before Mistress!"

She stood, exposing her knickers soiled with his cum.

"Lick that filth off me!"

"Yes, Mistress!"

Hubert licked her hand clean and then nuzzled his head between her thighs, sucking feverishly, his head reeling at the intimate fragrance of his new Domina's body.

"Take down Mistress's knickers!" Trembling hands eased them down.

Freya stepped out of them. "Pull them over your head!"

"Yes, Mistress!"

Hubert covered his face in their warm fragrance, his cock rising in renewed excitement.

"Filthy boy! You will wear Mistress's soiled knickers in bed to remind you of your disgusting behaviour. Return them nicely laundered next Saturday. Thank Mistress for your spanking and remain kneeling until Mistress has left the room!.

A muffled "Thank You, Mistress!" followed Freya to the door.

She stepped out, smiling triumphantly to the waiting Cordelia. "Are the horses saddled for us, darling?"

Postscript.

The Mistress of Camberley House and her attentive auburn-haired chaperone make a stunning pair as they canter side-saddle in Hyde Park's fashionable Rotten Row every Saturday morning. Gentlemen doff their hats to the elegantly attired ladies as they pass, little knowing that they are lovers and that Mistress always rides knickerless!

Company Policy
by Emily Dubberley

A new boy started working on my team at the office last month. Blond, tanned and tall; he thought he was it, wandering round in tight T-shirts, running his fingers through his hair with an implacable belief that every woman would find his tight, 22-year-old body irresistible. He also made it pretty clear that he was interested in me, despite the fact that he reported in to me. He'd linger by my desk, openly staring at my cleavage and making crude comments. I ignored him. I don't like men who think they're re god. I like men who worship me.

After a couple of weeks, it was getting hard to concentrate. He kept finding petty excuses to come and chat. It was flattering enough but every arrogant glance he shot at my thighs, made with the assumption that if I was *really* lucky, he might choose me for his bedmate, wound me up more and more.

By week three, he was clearly getting confused by my lack of response. He'd had offers from half the women in the company and had already screwed a lot of them but still, sheep-like, they gravitated towards him. I don't know if it was his youth, his arrogance or his body but something about him seemed to attract them. Idiots. I knew he was a shallow hump-and-dump merchant who clearly didn't know his place. But still he kept lingering by my desk. When he turned up with flowers for me on Friday, I'd had enough.

'Alex.'

'Yes…' His voice was tinged with hope.

'Your behaviour isn't appropriate for the office. Come to my office at 6pm. We need to talk through your future at this company.'

'But…'

'No buts. I said I'll talk to you at 6pm. Now get back to work.'

Someone had to show him the right way to treat a woman. I realised that it had to be me.

By 6pm, the office was practically empty. My team had won a big pitch so I'd sent them down to the pub to celebrate on my company credit card. Everyone else had headed off for the traditional Friday night drinks. Alex knocked on the door.

'Yes.'

He came in, looking nervous and started babbling.

'I'm really sorry, Ella. I really didn't think I was doing anything wrong. I'm sorry…'

'Shut up, Alex. What you did was inexcusable. Since you got here you've been staring at my tits and screwing your way around the office. Do you really think that's a professional way to behave?'

He blushed at my use of the word tits. 'No, Ella.'

'I think you need to be taught a lesson…'

'I'm really sorry.'

I shot an evil stare at him for interrupting.

'…about what women really want.'

His expression changed, as he thought about what I meant.

'And the first thing you're going to do is strip.'

He glanced nervously through the glass door of my

office.

'There are only the cleaners left in here and they won't be coming onto this floor for at least an hour. Didn't you hear what I said? Strip.'

He licked his lips, now dry with nerves and peeled off his tight white T-shirt to reveal a toned chest and six pack. I began to see his appeal.

'Now the rest.'

He unbuttoned his jeans and began to push them over his hips. I glared at him.

'Socks first. I was right. You know nothing.'

He blushed again and bent over to take off his socks. He hesitated and looked up at me to check that it was all right to remove the rest of his clothes.

'You may continue.'

He pushed his jeans down and stood in front of me wearing nothing but a tight pair of Calvin's. His cock was straining against them despite – or perhaps because – of the humiliation.

'And those!' I barked. 'Are you stupid?'

He slid them off to reveal a thick cock at least eight inches long and proudly erect. He tried to cover it, embarrassed at being aroused but I moved around the desk and slapped his hand away. 'You've been staring at me for long enough. What's the matter? Can't take it the other way round?'

He remained silent, clearly torn between embarrassment and arousal.

I pushed my skirt up to reveal my stockings and put one leg up onto a chair.

'Kneel down in front of me.'

He followed the order.

'Now lick my clit. Don't touch me with anything other than your tongue though or I'll have to punish you further.'

He looked ridiculous kneeling between my legs, craning

his neck forward as if bobbing for apples, but when his tongue touched my clit through my silk knickers, I had to grip on to the desk to keep my balance.

'Not bad. Make sure you lick my cunt thoroughly.'

He ran his tongue up and down my clit then moved down to my hole, sucking my juices through my knickers which were getting thoroughly wet. I grabbed the back of his head and pulled it into my crotch, grinding my clit into his face until I came hard. I kept hold of the back of his head until I'd recovered from my orgasm, then pushed him away, lowered my skirt and stood in front of him, looking calm.

'I suppose you're turned on now?'

'I want you, Ella.' He groaned.

'As you may have heard, I want, doesn't get. However, I am in need of some entertainment so…' I moved back to my desk and sat behind it, putting my legs up on the desk, crossed at the ankle to show him that he was the one putting on a show for me. 'You can wank for me.'

He looked as if he was going to cry, realising he was here to give pleasure, not get it.

'Come on!' I tapped my fingernails impatiently on the desk. He put his hand on his cock and started to pump it firmly, rubbing his thumb over its sensitive end.

'You'll have to be quicker than that. The cleaners will be here soon and I'm not letting you stop until you come, even if they do come in.'

It was a lie but I was getting bored and wanted to get home so that I could give myself a few more orgasms. I wasn't going to let him see me abandon myself that much.

He pumped harder and faster, clearly worried but desperate to come. His knees buckled and his cum spurted all over my desk, narrowly missing me.

'That was bad. You don't want the cleaners to know you've been wanking in the boss' office do you? You'd better lick it off.'

He looked flushed and ashamed as he knelt to lick my desk clean of his own cum. I enjoyed seeing the look on his face and would remember it later when I was alone.

'Right, all done then. Well, get your clothes on and hurry off home. I'm going to the bar to see the rest of the team. And if you're good next week, I may even let you go to the bar after you've finished too.'

'Next week?' His eyes were bright with excitement despite his clear anxiety.

'It takes more than one class to learn your lesson. Now, get out of my sight!'

My eyes followed his tight arse as he left my office. I smiled to myself, plans already formulating for next week's lesson.

The Hole In The Oak-Panelled Wall
by Roger Frank Selby

He carefully touched his left shoulder, expecting pain. It seemed fine, but he had this strong impression that he'd just hurt it. Weird! He shrugged and tried the door with his key. It opened.

The sight as he entered the room made him forget the shoulder in an instant. A woman knelt upon a small, carpeted platform. She was down on her hands and knees, but her head was out of sight – poked into a hole in the oak-panelled wall.

He moved closer. There was a collar-sized seal between her neck and the panel. How could her head have passed through – or how could it be pulled out again? But it didn't seem to trouble her – her spectacular body looked quite relaxed in her office clothes.

'Hello there, are you all right?'

Nothing.

'If you can hear me, pat the carpet.' He looked at her hands on the carpet. Very pretty hands. Well-kept nails and long fingers. Her slender arms led up to blouse-clad shoulders that leaned slightly against the oak. Wisps of very long black hair lay along her back, trapped in the neck-seal; separated from the rich tresses that must reach the floor in the next room.

Her left hand lifted, hesitated, then patted the carpet.

'Great, you can hear me! Right; one pat for "no"; two pats for "yes"... Do you understand?'

Two pats on the carpet

'You could be in quite a vulnerable position there.'

Three hard pats.

'I won't argue with that! Now, is there anything I can do to help you get free?'

One pat.

'Is there anything I *can* do for you?'

Two pats and then something else – her hand lifted to her waist. Her fingers fumbled at the top of her skirt and opened a zipper at her hip. Skin showed through the gap – creamy white skin. A sexual shockwave travelled downwards through his body.

'You want me to... Take off your skirt for you?'

Three hard pats and a voluptuous roll of her bottom that sent another bolt through his innards. He stood back, breathing deeply.

This was like some schoolboy fantasy. Had this woman deliberately placed herself in this vulnerable position where a passing stranger could take advantage? Apparently she had.

He approached the woman's rear end and touched the small of her back between grey skirt and white blouse, like a farmer checking if an animal was ready for service. Her waist dipped slightly as her bottom pushed up to him. This woman was ready. He eased the tight skirt over her behind and down.

'Now just a moment,' he said contemplating lace panties that barely covered the cheeks of her wide bottom, 'you have your hands free, couldn't you undress yourself?'

No reaction.

'I mean, it's a bit silly, me having to...'

She shuffled her knees closer to the wall to take all her weight. With both hands available she reached back to her skirt and pulled it up. A final zip, and she was fully dressed again.

Whatever she had wanted (and he was fairly sure what she'd wanted), he'd failed miserably in supplying it. 'Okay, so where do we go from here?'

She did not resume her previous inviting position, but sat back on her haunches – as far as she could, with her head through a wall.

'No hand signals then?'

Her hand lifted, but it didn't pat, it slowly waved goodbye.

Fucking fickle woman! His anger passed quickly – he knew he'd screwed up; hadn't been decisive enough. He'd be lucky to get a chance like *that* again. He fumbled for his key.

He let himself out through the exit door opposite the one he'd entered by. He tried the door that might bring him into the room where the woman's head ought to be.

It opened.

A similar room, and there was the woman's head poking through.

Blindfolded.

He was right about the hair. It reached to the floor and spilled over – a black cascade. She was beautiful – the blindfold couldn't hide high cheekbones and sensuous lips.

He could well imagine what she was going to say. A real put-down... Or maybe she would think he was a different man? Was that how this place worked? One thing he'd learned from his experience in the other room, it was best to say as little as possible, maybe nothing at all.

'Hello.' The sensuous lips were smiling.

He kept silent.

'I know you're here; I heard you come in. I can feel your presence, the warmth from your body, maybe.'

He stayed quiet.

'Pleased to meet you too. Are you having fun?' She waited. 'I'll take that to be a "no comment," then.

'Okay, you've decided not to talk and I can't say I blame you, considering the circumstances, but please let me know you're here, somehow. Whistle a tune or blow your nose or fart... Do all three if you like!'

He smiled for the first time. He knelt down and extended a hand towards her face. He gently touched her cheek and then traced the line of her jaw to her earlobe.

'That was... very nice... John. That will be your name. You can call me Jane – if you ever call me anything! Altogether you seem a touch too *romantic* for this place, but I guess you could say that this was the romantic side of the wall – I haven't thought about it before but that's the way it is.'

He tried to lift the blindfold.

'No, don't do that!'

It clung tightly to her face. A molecular bond of some kind...

'I want it on for now, anyway. Forget the blindfold; just keep talking to me in the language you're good at.'

He carefully took her face in both hands, angled it slightly to one side. Her lips parted a little and he glimpsed her waiting tongue. He kissed her. She responded, opening her mouth to him. He couldn't remember a kiss quite like it; he became lost in her moist warmth.

Her mouth remained slightly open afterwards, as she savoured the experience. 'Wow.'

He kissed her again, but halfway through she wiggled her face away. 'You may be a great kisser John, but there's someone in the room behind me!'

What? Someone else!

She sensed his surprise. 'There is. He just spoke to me. I can hear him, but he can't hear me. He wants to know if I'm all right.'

Although blindfolded, she looked distracted, concentrating on the voice he couldn't hear. She mumbled 'One pat for no, two for...'

Hey that's what *I* did! I guess it's not an unusual thing to do. He tried to listen to her.

She mumbled again. She didn't seem to be with him any more. He stood up and looked down at her. She tilted her head to one side, listening to the private voice. 'Of course I want my bloody skirt off, could I make it more obvious?'

He didn't want to hear this. This guy was probably going to succeed where he'd failed. Some people might find it a turn-on to listen to her end of the experience, with her (no doubt) describing the not-so-fine detail. He'd pass on that, thanks.

He glanced at the far end of the room. Another exit door. He used his key and left the room. It clicked shut.

He had to see just *who* it was in that first room, behind the wall. He had a strange idea who that might be in there with her...

He tried the door. Locked. If only he had...

Then he heard a noise inside the room – the sound of someone leaving through the far door? Maybe. He tried the key again. This time it worked.

There she was, alone. A woman he knew a little better. Jane. A wonderful kisser, with a body again. He could now visualise the complete woman – a real beauty! She was just as he'd left her before the other person came in, all zipped up. His rival had done no better than he.

Here was that lost opportunity again. This time it would be different! That lovely kiss had set the mood.

He got down beside her. 'Jane, it's me, John.' He *almost* added 'I'm here to do what you want me to do, we won't bother with any stupid hand signals.' But he kept his mouth shut and just stroked his hand along the groove of her spine until it rested on top of the double rise of her proud bottom.

She moved in reply, leaving him in no doubt. Her body-language was eloquent.

He unzipped her skirt and drew her clothing back and down, exposing her wonderful buttocks completely. Holding each cheek, he placed a kiss on each cool surface, followed up with a playful smack. From now on everything he did would be from his judgement of the woman he'd already met. Jane. A very sensuous person, not frightened of taking risks to explore her sexuality.

He reached around her, undoing buttons, brushing her taut brassiere with his hands. She lifted each arms in turn, helping to shed the blouse.

He surveyed her body. If there was any imperfection it was on the side of generosity – just like her mouth had been. Her bared bottom was perhaps slightly too rounded, and her covered breasts (Jane would call them boobs or even tits) a little on the generous side.

But she was in a hurry. Before he could do it, her hand lifted to the small of her back and slipped the hooks of her bra. Her breasts pushed out, jiggling invitingly as she lifted each arm to clear the straps away. He took her in his hands, gently kneading the soft flesh. She worked her shoulders with his handling. He could hear her moaning – the sound coming faintly through her body.

He cleared the lowered panties from her knees in a single movement. A kick of a leg and she was free of the clutter of clothing.

Her hand tugged at *his* clothes. After he'd shed them, her fingers found his cock, standing up well past the horizontal. He wished she could get both hands to him, or he get to her mouth, but she was directing the broad head to where nature intended it to go. She was wet. He heard her deep sigh as her pussy lips were separated and he pushed on smoothly into her depths, his spread fingers gripping the fullness of her bottom.

* * *

There she was, still wearing the blindfold, but not the big satisfied smile *he* was wearing.

'I suppose you're the twit who was in the room behind me just now?'

What?

'I'm surprised you have the nerve to show your face in here after such a pathetic performance!'

Hardly pathetic! He'd ridden her for ages, holding back as her muffled moaning grew louder, then finally coming at the same time as her, letting go with his explosive...

'OK, maybe that was a bit harsh, but you were so *boring*! All that self-justifying talk... I just had to wave goodbye.'

'But that was before!' He blurted out.

'Before what?'

'Before I kissed you.'

'Was that *you*? It couldn't have been! That was John; he's very nice. He's only just left. He left shortly after you started wasting my time. He never says anything but he really knows what a woman wants. You're all talk; all piss and wind...' She tensed. 'Oh my God! He's behind me now!

'But *I'm* John!'

'No, he just told me *he's* John – it's the first time he's spoken!

'But this is crazy!'

'Oh, shut up! Ah... He's just run his fingers down my spine. His hand is resting on... Oh Yes! That's what I want! Oh! He just pulled everything right down in one go – none of your pussyfooting antics! He has me bare-arsed in seconds!'

'But that's what *I* did!' Then suddenly he had it. He took her advice and shut up. She kept talking, whispering... Every action, every event, was as they'd recently performed – but not so recent that it didn't arouse him again.

'Jane,' he whispered as she began moaning softly, 'that's *me* behind you as well as in front, that's what I did to you twenty minutes ago.'

'What! How could it be?'

'I don't know, but how could I know your name. And *you* named me! And I tried to pull the blindfold off – then we kissed, twice. It was fantastic – but then we were interrupted – you said "You may be a great kisser John, but there's someone behind me..." That must have been my first visit to your body! That *was* a screw up! There seems to be some sort of time lag...'

But he'd lost her again. Where were they now? She had been mumbling and moaning about him feeling her tits, and now she sighed deeply... The cock was going in. He was fucking her... again!

'Aahh... Oohh... If you say so... John, I believe it's you, but he's... *You,* are deep inside me! John, kiss me again then I'll know...

He kissed her again – it wasn't quite the same kiss for him, with her being otherwise engaged, but she seemed to recognise it.

'John... Oh... I want you to do something more... Ah... I want you to put...'

'I know Jane, I'm ready...' He brushed the bulging cockhead against her cheek to show how ready he was. He was very gentle, offering her the tip against her lips. Her tongue crept out to lick him. Then her lovely lips parted for him and he carefully entered, aware how awkward it was for her without her hands and without much movement to control things. As it was, her head moved down on him with amazing freedom. She went on for a long time until he was ready, taking him in all the way, never jarring or forcing... Frequently with a rolling action, mirroring the way her bottom had moved – was moving right now as his other self also began to reach his culmination. The feeling of her lips and tongue working on him brought him to a climax again and he released into her mouth, her lips still sucking his shaft as she swallowed all he could spurt into her.

'So how does this finish? How do I get back to be one person? Do I just wait until I come through that entry door with a big smile on my face and join us? What then? Is it *"Zap!"* and I'm one person again?'

'No John, it couldn't be like that.' She seemed suddenly knowledgeable. 'There is *no way* you could meet yourself on this timeline. That would generate a paradox. You must leave by the exit door you used last time.'

'A paradox?' He'd read about those – something about going back in time and murdering an ancestor, so you couldn't have existed to do the deed in the first place – Hence the impossibility of time travel!

'Well, think back. You didn't see yourself in here twenty minutes ago, did you? If you came through that entry door now – as you did twenty minutes ago – you would have see you – but you didn't, did you?'

'I would have seen *myself*? No, I certainly didn't...' His eyes were glued on the door as if his earlier self was about to come marching in. Then he glanced down at her full lips – lips that had been lovingly sucking on him minutes earlier. 'Do you have a PhD in time travel or something?'

She smiled under the blindfold. 'Something like that.'

'And why the blindfold?'

'Haven't you worked that out yet? I'm just kinky!'

No. This was all too pat. 'Bullshit!' The whole set-up was now beginning to make sense – mundane commonsense. It was a clever deception, but suddenly he could see right through it. 'The blindfold is for my benefit! That was so I'd accept you not recognising that it was me again on my second Headroom visit... It would also help you in your acting.'

'Acting?'

'Yes – acting as though someone were behind you when I was servicing your head end!' He mimicked her voice: '"Oh, he's behind me now – I can hear him but you can't!" Time lag? Ha! What a load of crap! Of course the acting would be a lot easier if you had a male accomplice assisting you at the rear...' His contempt turned to anger. 'Yes! There must have been... for you to get everything exactly right, the timings... He must have been watching me on camera, and then giving you a second duplicate fucking...' He looked around wildly. 'Are there cameras in here too?'

'No, John! You've got it all wrong! Just *listen* to me for a second!'

'Go on then.'

'It's a very limited time distortion and it's only possible *because* you could put a conventional explanation on it. It *has* to be that way to avoid a dangerous paradox – or even a loop!'

'Oh *really?* Okay, now you listen to me.' His controlled anger was like an explosive device waiting to go off. 'I've done a little science too. A guiding principle is that the simplest explanation is usually the correct one: A hidden camera, a little acting and a willing accomplice – that's a far simpler explanation of the facts than bending time itself! '

'But not *this* time John.' she seemed to be getting very frightened. She must have touched a hidden control on the other side: the hole smoothly opened to the width of her shoulders. She pulled the rest of her body through to join him, removing the blindfold at the same time. Her eyes were a beautiful green, pupils dilated with alarm. Naked breasts angled out and bobbed as she moved, inner thighs glistening from recent sex.

'Don't try and distract me... *Jane.*' He dragged his eyes away and bent to peer cynically through the enlarged hole, into the other room. 'It looks normal enough in there – no accomplice, no other *me*, no *time* distortion. I suppose the other *time-lagged* me is waiting outside right now?' Was that terror in those green eyes?

She forced a smile. 'Look, we've had our fun. I'd really like to clean up now. There is no accomplice – and no *other* you!' She laughed, not very convincingly. 'You were right the first time, John – it was all my acting – just repeating what you'd done so beautifully before. You must leave by the exit door right now, but please come again sometime. You were terrific!'

'Don't snow me with flattery, I'm going to get to the bottom of this.' He marched back to the entry door and tried to open it.

Locked.

'Your accomplice *is* there; I can *sense* him... behind the door! Sod the lock, I'm going to force this fucking door!' He was a big man, once a useful rugby player. He stepped back a few paces.

'No! For God's sake John, *No!*'

As his shoulder crashed painfully into the splintering door he remembered the long wait outside – raised voices within. Then the sudden bursting of an angry man through the door – a man about his size... The screaming, naked beauty standing behind the man who cursed and held his shoulder; the man who looked just like..?

He carefully touched his left shoulder, expecting pain. It seemed fine, but he had this strong impression that he'd just hurt it. Weird! He shrugged and tried the door with his key. It opened.

The sight as he entered the room made him forget the shoulder in an instant. A woman knelt upon a small, carpeted platform. She was down on her hands and knees, but her head was out of sight – poked into a hole in the oak-panelled wall.

The Collaring Of Camilia
by Alexia Falkendown

My Diary. Cissbury Hall. 12 May, 1888.
............"Don't stop now! Don't stop! Yes! Yes! Suck it...my precious pearl!"

Mistress Augusta crushed me, smothering my head between her thighs as her orgasm mounted and broke like a wave crashing upon a shingle strand.

I sucked feverishly at her throbbing clitoris, gripping her bucking bottom as Mistress abandoned herself to her pleasure. She peaked, peaked and peaked again in an orgy of multiple orgasms, the delirium of her rapture convulsing us in her quivering ecstasy, as spasms of delight surged through her body.

Her frenzy passed, receding like the spent wave that leaves a glistening wetness upon an empty beach of broken shells.

Mistress's voice turned to a languid whisper. "Gently, now! Just lap me! Let me down gently! Caress it gently with your tongue. Kiss me!

Let me taste my love juices upon your lips! Cover me with your sweet soft body. Caress me softly...softly... Feel the faint reverberations, the dying echoes..."

Mistress released me to lie in blissful silence upon her sleeping body.

My sated pussy, that she had earlier ravished before the

assembled Sisters at my Collaring in the Temple, was now snugly pressed to her cunt. I had worshipped at last at Venus's portal. It was my nirvana. I was now absorbed into my Mistress's supreme spirit in ultimate submission as her chosen Handmaiden.

Delia paused in her reading and smiled at the precious memories evoked by her diary entry. Across the courtyard from her sumptuously furnished boudoir, the clock above Cissbury Hall's neo-classical portal whirred and struck midnight beneath a summer moon.

She bent and kissed the head of the girl sitting demurely at her feet.

"Queen Victoria celebrated her Golden Jubilee the year I made that entry. I was brought to Cissbury Hall six months earlier; an ignorant and angry orphan, spitting hatred for the Southwark workhouse from which Augusta had rescued me. In that short time she transformed me from a wild harpy into her loving and trusting Handmaiden – just as I have transformed you, my dearest Camilia, since rescuing you from that same workhouse and giving you a new name and life at my side."

She caressed Camilia's auburn curls. "I remember the journey from London vividly. It was a momentous event for me. '"Whip up! We have a train to catch for Brighton,' Augusta instructed the hansom cabbie waiting outside the workhouse as she bundled me inside. I had never set foot in cab or train before! At Victoria, Augusta found an empty 1st Class 'Ladies Only' compartment. I was nervously excited as the train steamed out of London. I was instantly attracted to this elegantly attired and handsome lady with long silver hair flowing unfashionably loose to the shoulder.

"No one, male or female, had ever affected me like that before and I was sensually aroused."

Returning to her diary, Delia found her description of that journey:

"I am Augusta, Chatelaine of Cissbury Hall, Abbess of the secret Sapphic Order of Cissbury Sybarites," she told me, as the train rolled through open countryside.

"You will feel at home with us. Some of our Sisters were once wild and angry girls like you. Your workhouse manager described you as a 'wild, vicious and untameable bitch', from which I deduce you fought off his filthy advances! He expressed his pleasure at seeing the back of you. The pleasure was doubtless mutual!"

Laying a possessive hand on my thigh, Augusta looked deep into my eyes. "So you see, my untamed beauty, I know all about you. And I am adept at gentling the wildest of animals. You are safe now. There is no drunken workhouse manager seeking to defile your femininity at Cissbury Hall. You will no longer be a victim of abuse, but a receiver of love, surrounded by Sisters and cared for by me, your very understanding Mistress."

She caressed my unkempt locks. "I shall name you Delia, after Goddess Diana of Delos. We have an altar to her in our Temple. Accept your good fortune, bow to my will and give yourself up to me as my chosen Handmaiden and I shall transform you into a poised, sophisticated and beautiful lady. I shall be your inspiration in all things. When I have tamed you, I shall collar you as my own and you shall share my bed and life. One day, when I am dead and buried, you yourself may become Abbess at Cissbury Hall. But first you must learn to please me and become the vessel of my will. It will be your deepest and most fulfilling goal to give up all control of your life and body to me. Do so, and I shall amply reward you with my love."

My stomach churned at this statuesque Domina's thrilling offer. I clutched her hand to my lips. "Thank you, for rescuing me from that hateful workhouse, Madame. I trust you and willingly accept your offer. Take me to your bosom and whip me into shape as your chosen

Handmaiden. I shall love you devotedly, submitting humbly and joyfully to your every whim."

"I am a kind, but strict Mistress," Augusta replied. "Once I have caressed the anger and hurt from your mind and body, you will become willingly receptive to my love cane's stinging caresses. There is truth in the epigram 'Spare the rod and spoil the pleasure!'" She squeezed my breast gently and my nipple hardened to her soft touch. A quiver of sexual arousal coursed through me.

She inclined her head and I felt the flicker of a serpentine tongue at my lips. I parted them in awakening desire. Her tongue became more insistent. An exploring hand slid up my inner thigh to caress the warmth of hidden delights. I opened my legs to her probing finger. It explored the wetness of my unaccustomed arousal, finding and tempting my clitoris from its hooded slumber. I moaned softly at her gentle, sensual touch; so delicate, so beautiful, so loving, so tender. The rough calloused hands of the gin-sodden workhouse manager, who had so often abused and attempted to rape me, were a forgotten nightmare.

The train's piercing whistle interrupted our intimacies.

"We have arrived at our destination. We shall continue this interesting 'conversation' elsewhere, when I can bring it to a more satisfying conclusion!" Lady Augusta smiled as she recovered her regal composure. "Open the carriage door, Delia, and hand me down. Sister Peneia awaits us with the brougham."

Delia put down her diary. "Thus began my new life with my late Mistress. It was an entrancing voyage of self-discovery and enlightenment as I gave my all in total submission to her. Having tamed and collared me, Mistress led me through intense physical and emotional climaxes of exquisite pain and delight. She took us both beyond this mundane world of sight, sound and feeling and into that nether realm of pure sensation and bonding where no culture, no society, no words stand between a caring Mistress and her chosen Handmaiden."

She gave Camilia her hand to kiss. "Yours will be a similar lifetime of discovery as my chosen Handmaiden. And now it's past midnight, my dear. Retire to your bed! You must prepare for our full-moon Temple ritual tomorrow when you take your vows of submission to me and I replace your leather training collar with one of gold. Tomorrow, I shall take you at last to my love bed as my Sapphic Collarbride."

Camilia pressed her Mistress's hand to her lips and silently left her boudoir.

The neo-classical Rotunda designed for Lord Cissbury by James Wyatt in 1790 as an adjunct to Cissbury Hall is a miniature copy of his famous London Pantheon, now sadly demolished. The rotunda, placed in a picturesque Capability Brown landscape overlooking the lake fronting the Hall, was designed to provide a suitable venue for Regency revelry.

When, as a rich young widow, Lady Augusta had inherited the Hall and parkland half a century later, she determined to turn it into the rural retreat for her secret Sapphic group devoted to promoting an independent lifestyle for women, and she settled the property in perpetuity on its members. Restricting their numbers to twelve Dominas and their chosen Handmaidens, they call themselves, to this day, the Cissbury Sybarites.

The Rotunda, with its gleaming pink and white marbled interior, was perfect for their secret Sybaritic ceremonies and sensual Sapphic rituals. Augusta lost no time in filling it with suitably erotic Classical and Renaissance statues of Venus, Astarte, Diana, Aphrodite, Hecate, and Nemesis brought from Greece, Rome and Florence. At their Temple dedication, the Cissbury Sybarites proclaimed their founding benefactress 'Abbess' and temple 'High Priestess'; duties assumed by Delia upon Augusta's death.

For Camilia's Collaring, the Temple was bathed in mellow candlelight that illuminated the statues and flower-bedecked altars. A richly accoutred Submission-bed with tether posts stood prominently in the centre.

The Cissbury Sybarites assembled there at moonrise, each leading a leashed and collared Handmaiden. They were naked beneath their long white satin robes which shimmered in the flickering candlelight. They stood facing the Venus altar served by an acolyte tending a small copper brazier glowing with coals onto which she threw dried jasmine blossoms. A filigree collar of braided Welsh gold, two gold rings and an ornately decorated parchment scroll, signed earlier that day, lay on the altar.

The acolyte sounded a gong. The Temple doors opened and Delia entered, attended by Camilia at heel on a leash attached to her training collar. Her normally loose auburn hair was pulled back and plaited into a ponytail wound and secured on top of her head, accentuating the delicate curve of her neck and her wide leather training collar. Delia led her to the altar and turned her to face the assembly. Camilia stood in an emerald-green silk dress, tied at the shoulders.

Delia unleashed her and removed her collar.

"Stand!"

Camilia placed her hands on her head. Her Mistress undid the bows of her dress, letting the ends drop. The dress slid down, caught momentarily on the fullness of her uplifted breasts as if reluctant to leave her body, before slithering over her pink nipples in their powder-puff aureoles to fall to the floor. Her oiled body revealed a smoothly shaven, virginal *mons veneris;* a picture of seductive naked beauty that brought a murmur of admiration from the assembled Sisterhood.

"Preen!"

Camilia ran her hands sensuously over her nakedness, enjoying the admiring gazes as she cupped her thrusting breasts, lingered to tweak her nipples into hardness before descending to caress her pink virginity. She looked voluptuously feminine and desirable in her nudity. She smiled; Mistress's radiant virgin Collarbride of Sappho!

"Kneel!"

Delia's sharp command brought Camilia's clit-fingering to an abrupt end. She knelt and faced the altar.

The acolyte handed the scroll to her. In a voice choking with emotion, she read out the words of her Submission:

<u>Collaring Contract of the Cissbury Sybarites</u>

The Goddess of a Thousand Names is Creatress of the Universe.

In Mistress Delia is the sacred form of the Goddess Eternal.

Handmaiden Camilia places her life and wellbeing in the hands of Mistress Delia and acknowledges her as Mistress in all things.

Handmaiden Camilia promises to honour, obey, please, adore, and worship her Mistress together with the sanctity of her body as a Divine Incarnation of The Goddess.

There are not, nor have been, nor shall be, any riches more precious to Handmaiden Camilia than the love and approval of her Mistress.

There is no pleasure for Handmaiden Camilia to equal that of offering her body to her Mistress.

There is no jewel more precious to Handmaiden Camilia than the Mistress's hallowed clitoral pearl that lies within the sacred oyster of Her Divine Venus.

There is not, nor has been, nor shall be, any orgasmic ecstasy for Handmaiden Camilia that can compare with her Mistress, nor mystical formula nor feminine sensuality to match her.

Handmaiden Camilia accepts with humble adoration and constant desire, the physical manifestation of her Mistress Domina's love; that sacred bond of pain and pleasure that Mistress metes out to her with love cane, tawse, flogger, hand and mouth.

Handmaiden Camilia freely chooses this destiny in the certain knowledge that she is the totally Beloved of her Mistress in Word, Deed and Spirit until the end of Time.

Camilia affixes her signature to this contract before the Goddess in binding submission as Mistress's chosen Handmaiden.

Signed: Camilia of Cissbury, Handmaiden. *Witnessed: Delia of Cissbury,* Mistress.

Camilia rose and placed the parchment on the altar. Taking a handful of jasmine blossoms, she sprinkled them on the brazier coals and raised her arms in silent orison. As the fragrant incense rose to the Goddess, she turned to kneel again before her Mistress.

"Camilia humbly beseeches Mistress to collar and purify her, that all may see her humbly devoted dedication as Mistress's chosen Handmaiden."

The acolyte handed Delia the golden collar. Placing it around Camilia's neck, she intoned: "I collar you, Camilia, as a symbol of your submission and obedience to me as my chosen Handmaiden.

In return, I, Delia, your Abbess and High Priestess do swear that I shall love and care for you as your Protectress in all things at all times."

Taking the two gold rings from the acolyte's hand she placed one on Camilia's wedding finger and the other on her own. "We wear our rings as a symbol of our shared love, commitment and bond between Mistress and her chosen Handmaiden."

Discarding her open robe Delia stood in flawless nakedness; a proud Domina looking down at her collared

Handmaiden. The acolyte handed Camilia a double dildo and harness. She put the alter-dildo to her lips and sucked it like a cock. Having moistened it, she pressed it to her Mistress's cunt, reverently parting her labia to ease it snugly into her receptive vagina. She buckled the harness around Delia's hips and thighs, pulling the straps tight. The eight inch leather cock stood proudly erect.

Delia raised Camilia to her feet, and led her over to the altar of Nemesis, Goddess of the Scourge. A thin cane and a flogger lay there. Taking up the cane, she flexed it and turned to her Handmaiden.

"Kiss this sacred scourge with which I shall purify your body!"

Camilia reverently kissed the rod and the hand that held it. "Whip me, Mistress! Whip your loving Handmaiden!" She moved to the Nemesis altar fashioned like a punishment block for temple scourging and bent over it.

"Present your bottom for punishment!"

Camilia spread her legs to part her bottom cheeks, arched her back and 'presented' her sweet peachy spheres to the gaze of her Domina. Delia could see the pink tightness of her puckered sphincter and, below it, peeping out from beneath the undercurve of her rounded bottom, the swollen love lips that would later submit to her proudly erect cunt cock. Her full breasts dangled over the altar's side and swung in pendulous freedom.

There was total silence in the temple's sexually charged air. Camilia felt a lingering caress, a soft touch at her pudenda, a gentle finger at the puffy lips of her moistly welcoming slit, exploring her inner labia, teasing her clit to throbbing arousal. She waited with bated breath.

Crack!

Camilia screamed as the cane seared across the spheres of her splayed cheeks with a crack like Jove's lightning bolt. Two more strokes burned their fiery lines of pain across Camilia's quivering bottom before Mistress caressed the raised crimson welts and called upon her to rise, kiss her cane in gratitude and place it on the altar. Delia kissed away a tear from Camilia's eye, picked up the flogger and led her back to kneel before the Venus altar.

"Beg!"

Camilia cupped her breasts invitingly, wiggled her now burning butt, and whined appealingly; a perfect picture of handmaidenly supplication.

Delia placed a hand on Camilia's head and thrust her pelvis out provocatively.

"Suck!"

She gripped Delia's leather shaft and sucked, taking it deep into her throat until she was almost gagging.

"Lie!"

Camilia ceased her deep-throating of Mistress's glistening shaft and mounted the Submission-bed to lie in supine expectancy, pelvis raised by a central cushion, her virgin pussy moistly open. Delia picked up the tethers and secured Camilia's limbs firmly to the corner posts. She turned and addressed the assembled Sisterhood who had reached a fever pitch of arousal at the unfolding ritual.

"Handmaiden Camilia has demonstrated Obedience. She has accepted the Sacred Scourging of our Order.

"She will now demonstrate her delight at my flogger's caresses to her bountiful breasts and succulent pussy, bared so invitingly to our gaze. She must arouse me with her cries and moans before begging me to deflower her before the Goddess. When I have breached her maidenhead, I shall fuck her newly opened vagina slowly and sensuously, just as you will later fuck your own Handmaidens assembled here tonight to celebrate Camilia's Collaring."

Delia masturbated her dildo as she spoke, enjoying the spasms of pleasure in her tightly-filled cunt as she vibrated it. A quiver of anticipatory pleasure rippled through

Camilia's tethered body as she squirmed against her restraints. Her clitoris now throbbed within its moist conch, the swollen love-bud peeking out of its protective hood, inviting Mistress's attention.

Spread-eagled, with her nakedness presented to the aroused gaze of her Sisters, Camilia felt totally vulnerable, deliciously powerless, unable to resist the sacred progression of Submission and Defloration by her adored Mistress. She wriggled her hips and rounded up-thrust breasts provocatively, invitingly, straining against her bonds in mute desire, begging to be temple-flogged, taken and ravished.

A seated acolyte began to drum, her fingers softly beating out a tattoo on the stretched skin.

Delia slowly drew her flogger's soft leather falls over Camilia's exposed cunt lips, belly and breasts, then to her moaning lips.

"Kiss the leather that will whip you!"

Camilia savoured the leather's smell as Delia dragged the falls slowly over her face, kissing them as they slithered over her lips. And suddenly Delia's own lips were upon hers in a whispered endearment of tender love.

"I love you," Camilia breathed softly back.

Delia stood back out of her Handmaiden's line of sight and ran her fingers through the flogger's falls. Camilia arched her back expectantly, thrusting her breasts up provocatively. The beating drum took on a more urgent pace.

Thwack!

The flogger's tails arced down. "Oooh!" Camilia grunted throatily as the leather fingers kissed her open pussy lips and her inner thighs' vulnerable tenderness.

Thwack!

"Aaah! Yes!"

The leather tails visited the inviting cunt lips again,

splaying out in stinging caress.

Thwack!

"Ooooh! Mmmmmmm!" The stinging strokes upon her exposed love lips brought tears to Camilia's eyes and she wriggled her pelvis, displaying the wet pinkness of her vulnerable virginity.

"Fuck me now, Mistress! Fuck me! Make me your Sacred Whore!"

Thwack!

"Aaaaaaaaah!" Another stinging blow descended on her pussy. Delia allowed the tails to lie a moment before dragging them over her body to Camilia's lips.

"Kiss the leather!"

Camilia responded, smelling the heady mixture of her cunt juices on the aromatic tresses.

Delia moved round to stroke her Handmaiden's now reddened *mons veneris*, feeling the flowing moistness of arousal as she fingered the succulence of her throbbing pearl.

"I love you!" Delia whispered. She raised her flogger and struck higher to sting Camilia's up-thrust breasts.

Thwack! Thwack!

"Aaaaaaaaaaaaaah!" Camilia squirmed beneath this new attack. Pain mixed with mounting desire gripped her. She whimpered, pleading with her Mistress to stop, while thrusting her breasts up to receive the flogger's salacious caress.

Thwack! Thwack!

Camilia closed her eyes, yielding to the stinging joy of the leather's tit-strokes. Her breasts felt as if they would explode to the frenetic beat of the drum-led flogger.

She was suddenly aware of a new sensation. Fingers parted her cunt lips to expose the fleshy redness of her waiting virginity with its moistly throbbing clitoral bud. A serpentine tongue flicked at her musky strawberry. Two lips closed on it, nibbled and sucked. She moaned softly and opened her eyes to watch her Mistress lover feed at her cunt and sip from her sacred chalice.

"Drink me Mistress! Sup at my table! Devour me utterly! Take my virginity!"

Camilia strained at her ankle bonds to give greater access to her Goddess portal. She felt the hard dildo cock head press against her cunt. She groaned, gasping as the majesty of its seemingly massive girth battered at her hymen. Her portal stretched to accommodate Delia's shaft in its tight, welcoming embrace. Delia slid her lance out, thrust hard in, and still further in. Camilia grunted at the onslaught's impact. Beads of sweat broke upon her brow. She felt a stab of sudden pain as her hymen broke.

"Take It, Mistress! Take It! Take my Gift! Enter your Love temple!"

Mistress's pace quickened to her Handmaiden's exhortations. Delia clutched at Camilia's bursting tits, covering her with passionate kisses as she forced her cunt cock home to the full length of its leather shaft, tearing at last through Camilia's maidenhead in a final fiery love thrust.

The drumming reached a crescendo. Mistress began to fuck hard, fuck deep, fuck fast.

"Aaaah –Aah! Aaaah – Aah! Camilia grunted at each stroke, writhing in rhythmic delirium to cock and drum.

"Fuck me! Fuck me! Goddess-Bitch! Make me cum!"

She wanted to tear Delia's back with her nails as the ecstasy began to build deep within her belly, but the tethers held her immobile. She could do nothing but lie there and be ravished as the throbbing sound of Temple drumming washed over her again and again. A streak of blood coursed from her portal onto the towel beneath her as Delia pumped her hips, her cunt cock pistoning in and out in a rampant rhythm that massaged and titillated both Mistress and

Maiden.

Camilia's pain at her torn hymen was lost beneath her growing euphoria as her Mistress's now bloodied weapon throbbed through her body.

"Aaah –Aah! Aaah – Aah! Grind me! Fuck me! Fill me!" she shouted, urging her rider on.

Delia felt her orgasm building as the beat-beat-beat of the drum enflamed their mutual passion. She thrust ever faster, taking her Handmaiden with her to the pinnacle. Her orgasm mounted with each determined thrust – a throbbing glow that transmitted itself to her pinioned mount. Camilia began to shudder beneath her as her climax brimmed and overflowed, sweeping all feeling before it, surging through her body in waves of ecstasy. She quivered uncontrollably, as the orgasmic charge coursed through every nerve of her body.

Delia's own climax came as the temple drumbeat rose to a final deafening crescendo. She collapsed onto her Handmaiden, cunt to cunt, breast to breast, lips to lips, tongue entwined with tongue in impassioned kiss. Clutching Camilia's tortured bottom, Delia began a slow, dreamlike grind; a gentle barely perceptible rhythmic rocking that milked the last orgasmic sensations from their enraptured bodies. The last echo faded and Mistress was still, her leather muscle embedded deep inside Camilia's sacred portal. Handmaiden lay silently comatose beneath her. Drained! Deflowered! Ravished! Radiant!

Mistress and maiden were awakened from their orgasmic reverie by an appreciative round of applause from their mesmerized audience. Delia rose, extracting her embedded cunt cock from her Handmaiden's ravished pussy. She gently pulled the bloodied silk towel from beneath Camilia's striped bottom and rubbed the dildo clean of blood and vaginal juices. She and her Handmaiden would make a burnt offering of the blood-soaked towel as a thanksgiving to the Goddess on the morrow.

Delia unfastened Camilia's tethers, and helped her from the now sanctified Submission-bed.

"Unstrap my dildo, darling, and follow me! The night is yet young! We shall leave our Sisters to their own rituals and continue our worship of Venus in private. Your ultimate submission has only just begun!"

Mistress Domina Delia took Camilia's hand, pausing to collect the cane from the Nemesis altar on their way out.

Imagine great sex on your doormat every month!

- Imagine a new Xcite book landing on your door mat every month.
- Imagine reading the twenty varied and exciting stories that each book contains.
- Imagine that three books are absolutely FREE as is the postage and packing.

No hassles
No shopping
Just pure fun

Yes! that's the Xcite subscription deal –
for just £69.99 (a saving of over £25) you will get 12 books
with free P&P delivered by Royal Mail (UK addresses only)

All books are discreetly and perfectly packaged
Credit cards are billed to Accent Press ltd

Order now at www.xcitebooks.com
or call 01443 710930

JoyBear
PICTURES
Play together!

'If, as a couple, you have not watched an erotic film together this would be a perfect opportunity to dip your toe gently in.'

Scarlet Magazine

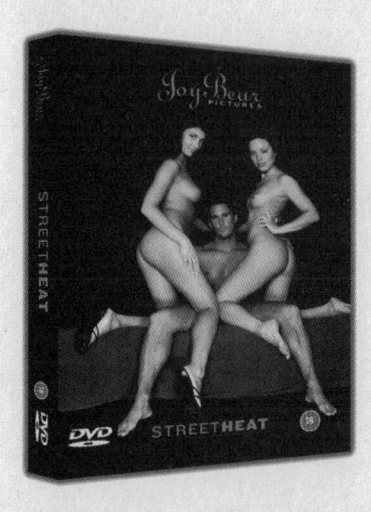

Erotic Films on demand

Watch now by logging onto:

www.joybear.com

Special Online Offer for Xcite Readers!

All our films online are split into scenes, giving you greater choice and DVD quality. We are delighted to present Xcite readers with a special buy one get one free offer. Simply choose any two scenes and we will only charge you for one. Please enter the promotional code below when prompted:

XCITEJOY01

Also available from Xcite Books:
(www.xcitebooks.com)

Sex & Seduction 1905170785 price £7.99
Sex & Satisfaction 1905170777 price £7.99
Sex & Submission 1905170793 price £7.99

5 Minute Fantasies 1 1905170610 price £7.99
5 Minute Fantasies 2 190517070X price £7.99
5 Minute Fantasies 3 1905170718 price £7.99

Whip Me 1905170920 price £7.99
Spank Me 1905170939 price £7.99
Tie Me Up 1905170947 price £7.99

Ultimate Sins 1905170599 price £7.99
Ultimate Sex 1905170955 price £7.99
Ultimate Submission 1905170963 price £7.99